With two beautiful daughters, **Lucy Ryder** has had to curb her adventurous spirit and settle down. But, because she's easily bored by routine, she's turned to writing as a creative outlet, and to romances because— 'What else is there other than chocolate?' Characterised by friends and family as a romantic cynic, Lucy can't write serious stuff to save her life. She loves creating characters who are funny, romantic and just a little cynical.

Also by Lucy Ryder

Resisting Her Rebel Hero
Tamed by Her Army Doc's Touch
Falling at the Surgeon's Feet
Caught in a Storm of Passion

Rebels of Port St. John's miniseries

Rebel Doc on Her Doorstep

Discover more at millsandboon.co.uk.

REBEL DOC ON HER DOORSTEP

BY
LUCY RYDER

MILLS & BOON

First published in Great Britain 2017
by Mills & Boon, an imprint of HarperCollins*Publishers*
1 London Bridge Street, London, SE1 9GF

Large Print edition 2018

ISBN: 978-0-263-07258-7

MIX
Paper from
responsible sources
FSC
www.fsc.org   FSC C007454

This book is produced from independently certified FSC™ paper to ensure responsible forest management. For more information visit www.harpercollins.co.uk/green.

Printed and bound in Great Britain
by CPI Group (UK) Ltd, Croydon, CR0 4YY

34756140

This book is dedicated to my great-niece
Coral-Mae, who was born during a screaming
deadline. Excellent timing, kiddo, but
you've brought such joy to us all. We really
look forward to all those weekly photos.

And also to my nephew, Jason,
who has just graduated cum laude.
Congrats to our very own Dr Jay Bass.

CHAPTER ONE

DR. PAIGE CARLYLE jolted awake from her first decent sleep in over a week. One minute she was dreaming about lying on the deck of a sleek boat while a hot captain rubbed oil all over her body, the next...nightmare city. Frozen with fright, Paige strained for the noise that had awakened her. Vaguely aware that her heart was pounding like that of an overexcited kid pigging out on Halloween candy, she held her breath until... There, she thought when the sound came again. There it is. A heavy thud followed by...cursing?

In the darkness her eyes widened and her heart rate doubled, banging against her ribs like it was practicing for a world heavyweight title.

You have got to be kidding me!

An intruder?

What the heck had happened to the Chamber of Commerce's pledge that crime was non-existent in Port St. John's? What about her landlord's blithe assurances that she could sleep with her doors unlocked?

Yeah, right, she snorted. Try telling that to her intruder.

A large *male* intruder by the sounds of it.

Had she locked the front door? The sliding French doors leading to the deck? *Dammit,* she couldn't remember. But she'd been in the seaside town eight months and hadn't developed any reckless habits of leaving everything unlocked, so she was almost certain she had.

But "almost" wasn't certain enough, she told herself frantically. Not when a woman's worst nightmare was about to unfold. *Oh, God.* Not when she didn't have a weapon to defend herself with.

Why hadn't she just stayed in the city where everyone locked themselves behind thick doors and deadbolts? Yeah, and while she was at it, why hadn't she just robbed a bank to pay for med school instead of signing her life away on a scholarship?

If she had she wouldn't be here now. Instead of paying off her debt, she'd be working as a pediatrician. Probably from behind bars but, what the heck, at least she wouldn't be—

Black dots began to appear in her vision and she realized she was still holding her breath. Expelling it on a quiet rush, Paige tossed back the covers and eased to the edge of the bed, searching in the dark for her cellphone.

It wasn't there and for one panicked moment she couldn't remember where she'd left it... Instead, her hand came into contact with a heavy flashlight she'd used a few nights earlier when they'd had a blackout.

Okay. Weapon? Check.

Nerve? Oh, boy.

With the heavy weight in her hand, her head cleared enough to recall the brotherly advice she'd received over the years. But actually doing it was a far cry from practicing on three hulking males who thought it hysterically funny to simply put a big hand on her head and hold her an arm's length away while she "practiced" taking them down.

Bolstered by the fact that she knew a few badass moves and could totally defend herself—she hoped—Paige breathed in and out a few times then headed for the door. She carefully poked her head into the passage, swallowing a squeak of terror when she heard a crash and another round of inventive cursing.

Gulping, she slapped a hand over her galloping heart before it crashed right through her ribs and went tearing off down the stairs, probably to escape out the front door.

Oh, yeah. She was totally kicking this badass thing.

But that was okay, she thought, lifting the flashlight like a baseball bat and giving it a practice swing. The flashlight could probably crush a skull or break a kneecap. Maybe. Probably…in the hands of someone weighing more than one twenty-five soaking wet…but it was all she had.

Tiptoeing to the landing, Paige peered over the railing where light from a nearby streetlamp shone through the stained-glass door inset, illuminating the entrance like a church. She hoped it wasn't a sign that she was about to sing with the angels.

Squaring her shoulders, Paige descended the stairs, bare feet silent on the treads, muscles tensed in preparation for a quick getaway through the front door, and…rolled her eyes.

Look at her, all brave and fierce.

If her brothers could see her now they'd probably die laughing. Or disown her.

There was another loud thud and a couple of beats later a round of pithy curses. Huffing out a breath that disturbed tendrils of wild bed hair, Paige tightened her grip on the flashlight and reached for the landline phone mounted on the wall. She heard the voice of the 911 operator in her ear asking about her emergency and it took a few seconds to realize the intruder was moving again. Towards her.

Eek.

She caught a brief glimpse of a huge black shadow, arm outstretched like the walking dead, and before she could stop herself she opened her mouth and let rip with a scream worthy of a B-grade slasher flick.

The hulk stopped, swayed for a second before shoving out a hand to steady himself against the wall. A deep voice snarled, "What the—? Who the hell are you?"

She let out another shriek and reacted by heaving the heavy flashlight at him. She heard it connect solidly, he gave a soft grunt, and the next second toppled. Just like a giant redwood. *Whomp!* Landing hard enough to shake the earth.

For several long moments he didn't move and neither did Paige as the flashlight spun in crazy circles on the wooden floor. The impact must have switched it on and with each rotation its beam briefly illuminated the man lying face down on her entrance floor.

Just like a corpse on TV.

When he remained motionless, Paige grabbed the flashlight mid-spin and trained the beam on him, ready to whack him if he so much as twitched.

Beam wobbling in her sweaty grasp, she edged closer and gingerly stretched out a leg to poke him with her foot. He gave a low groan and she jumped back, a strangled squeak catching in her throat.

After a minute of nothing but Paige's ragged breathing, she prodded him a bit harder. Okay, so it was more of a kick but she needed to make sure he wasn't lulling her into a false sense of security before grabbing her and giving her a coronary before she turned thirty.

When he didn't move or make any more creepy sounds, she leaned a little closer...and... *Holy cow...*sucked in a shocked breath.

He was gorgeous.

At least what she could see of him under all the scrapes and bruises. She didn't know what she'd expected an intruder to look like, but *yeesh*, gorgeous wasn't it.

Damn. What a waste of man candy.

Had she...?

Her heart skipped a couple of beats until she saw that his right hand and arm was encased in a cast. Exhaling in a gusty whoosh, she decided that no way had she done all that. Besides, she was five-five and he was...over six feet...and solid looking. Big enough to squash her like a bug if she hadn't panicked and thrown the flashlight at him.

He was all hard angles and masculine power, with the face of a warrior angel...fierce and awesome male beauty relaxed in...

Paige gulped.

Oh gosh, she thought a little hysterically, had she just killed the hottest guy in the northern hemisphere? A guy who looked like he'd gone a couple of rounds with the Exterminator and survived. Only to be felled by a...a—

Reality finally hit her and she sagged against the wall, a shaky laugh escaping. It was filled with more than a little hysteria because... *Wow.* She'd done it. She'd totally taken out the bad guy.

In her head she did a little victory dance. She was *awesome! Who's the girl? Who's the—?*

From down a long tunnel she heard a tinny voice telling her to remain calm, that the police were on their way. Baffled, Paige looked around and noticed the receiver hanging from the wall unit by a long spiral cord. And blinked.

Oh. Right—911.

Eyes locked on the hot guy, she fumbled the receiver with shaking hands and lifted it to her ear, managing to whack herself on the cheek in the process.

"Ouch."

"Hello, ma'am. Ma'am, can you hear me? The police are on their way. Are you hurt?"

Blinking back tears that were most likely from fear and the massive doses of adrenaline still pumping through her system, Paige managed to croak out, "N-no, I'm n-not hurt. But I'm p-pretty sure I just k-k-killed the hot guy."

Her breath escaped in a loud *whoosh*. A seriously hot guy came willingly into her house and what did she do? She killed him, that's what, she thought with a splutter of hysterical laughter. Frankie was going to disown her.

Dr. Tyler Reese swam up through thick layers of consciousness aware of a vicious pounding in his head. Having recently become familiar with the sensation, he let out a rough groan, thinking he was back in the ER after his accident.

A low husky voice ordered him not to move but he disregarded it and lifted a hand to his head before recalling that his arm was encased in a cast from elbow to knuckles. And the move had him sucking in a sharp breath of agony that had nothing to do with his headache.

"I told you not to move," the voice said, sounding a little exasperated. "And use the other hand before you give yourself another bruise. But I warn you. Try anything funny, and it's lights out."

His head pounded harder and a burning pain radiated out from his shoulder. He knew without being told he'd dislocated it—especially as the pain was accompanied by the almost overwhelming urge to toss his cookies.

Wasn't that just freaking peachy? Another damn injury to add to the ones he'd recently acquired.

"What the—?" he slurred, prying open his lids and blinking up into the faces swimming a couple of inches above him. Faces that looked remarkably like...faeries? He blinked again and two momentarily became one.

Yep. A freaking crazy-haired faerie. Although what the hell one was doing almost cross-eyed half an inch from his face was something he wasn't ready to contemplate.

He narrowed his gaze until his vision cleared, revealing a faerie that was more likely to grace the pages of a graphic novel than a children's bedtime story book—which meant he was hallucinating and his mild concussion had just been bumped up to serious head trauma.

Realizing he was scowling up at her, she gave a startled squeak and scuttled out of sight—too fast to see if she had any wings. The sudden move made him dizzy so he closed his eyes to prevent a brain aneurysm and gave a silent snarl.

Great. Just freaking perfect. His life officially sucked. He'd escaped an aggressive drunk intent on mowing him down only to be felled by a pint-sized attacker intent on splitting his head open like a watermelon.

What the hell had he done to deserve this?

His musings were interrupted by a soft sound of throat-clearing and a shaky but peremptory, "Hey."

He cracked open an eye and mulled over the fact that she was still there, and couldn't decide if it was good or very bad. Good that he wasn't hallu-cinating and bad because…yep, there was still a wild-haired, wide-eyed faerie staring at him like he'd crash-landed in her flower patch.

Then he spotted the flashlight raised ready to bean him if he so much as twitched and he decided that if he *was* hallucinating she would be dressed in gossamer wisps, not a huge ratty old USMC T-shirt, looking fierce and crazy and ready to inflict more pain.

His heavy sigh emerged as a low groan. *So much for that fantasy.* He'd finally lost his mind if the sight of this wild exotic creature made him want to smile when he had absolutely nothing to smile about. His surgical career might very well be over thanks to a drunk who'd sideswiped him, leaving him with broken carpals and ulna in his dominant hand, along with damaged ligaments.

Suddenly his well-ordered life had been invaded by a horde of women eager to take care of him and to escape the chaos he'd packed a bag and headed for the one place on the planet he'd been happy— his father's house on the Olympic Peninsula.

It had been an impulsive decision but Ty wanted to be alone. What better place than his childhood getaway in Port St. John's? He'd spent summers here escaping from the rigidly stifling atmosphere of his mother's house until he'd turned eighteen.

Maybe he should have called first, but his battery had died and, frankly, it hadn't even occurred to him that Henry Chapman wouldn't be home.

Or that he'd be attacked by a wild faerie commando barely reaching his chin. It was humiliating, *dammit*. He just hoped his friends never found out or he'd never live it down.

And another thing—what the hell was this creature doing in his father's house?

He pushed up with his good arm, intending to demand answers, and promptly froze when pain had him sucking in an agonized breath. Sweat popped out on his forehead and he was forced to sag embarrassingly against the nearest wall to breathe past the nausea.

"Who...are...you?" he gritted out in a voice guaranteed to send hospital staff running. "And what the hell did you throw at me?"

The faerie arched her brow at him as though he was a grumpy adolescent who'd momentarily forgotten his manners. "You first," she said, with only a hint of a quiver in her voice.

It both irritated and earned his reluctant admiration because it took guts to hold off a guy almost a foot taller and a hundred pounds heavier with nothing but a firm little chin, a steely-eyed stare and a flashlight. All while dressed in nothing but a huge, faded T-shirt and a kick-ass attitude.

That mouth—wide, lush and soft—was another matter altogether. A mouth like that gave a man ideas. Ideas that would probably earn him another concussion.

"That way we can get the introductions out of the way before I inflict any more pain on you," her mouth said, completely destroying the fantasy forming in his head.

He squinted at her silently for a couple of beats before looking pointedly at the flashlight. "Thinking of giving me concussion?" He gave a hard laugh. "Hate to rain on your parade, babe, but some idiot already beat you to it."

"No," she said, gesturing to his shoulder with a jerk of her chin. "I'm going to reset your shoulder, *babe*. You dislocated it when you took a header into the floor."

Her tone suggested he was an idiot, which irritated the hell out of him enough that he tersely pointed out, "Which I wouldn't have done if you hadn't tried to split my skull open like a watermelon."

"Which *I* wouldn't have done if you hadn't broken into my house and scared me half to death," she retorted just as shortly, visibly relaxing when they heard a car screeching to a stop outside. Car doors slammed and there was the sound of boots thudding up the stairs, then a brisk knock at the door.

"The cops?" he demanded, outraged. "You called the damn cops?" He knew he was being unfair, but the whole situation was surreal, taking him back to the last time he'd been in this Washington seaside town, beaten up and in trouble with the cops because he and his buddies had thought they had something to prove in a bar filled with local roughnecks.

He'd just turned eighteen and had wanted to flex his I'm-now-officially-cool muscles. He vividly remembered standing in a jail cell while his mother had coldly and furiously berated his father for not keeping Ty on a short leash.

Yeah, right. Henry Chapman had worked all the time and as long as Ty hadn't ended up in his ER, he'd pretty much trusted him to stay out of trouble.

That had been the last time he'd spent summers in Port St. John's because he'd been in med school and then establishing his surgical career, but mostly because he'd been mad at Henry for not standing up to Ty's mother. For not fighting for a relationship with his son.

It had been pretty juvenile but if his recent accident had taught him anything it was that life could be snuffed out in an instant and it was time to mend his relationship with his father.

He was distracted from his inner musings when he caught her over-the-shoulder glance that suggested his IQ was lower than a rock's. It didn't faze him because, let's face it, it wasn't the first time he'd been an idiot. He'd thought he'd outgrown his impulsive tendencies but apparently not or he'd never have hopped on the first flight into SEATAC airport and headed for the Olympic Peninsula.

He didn't know what he'd been thinking because it hadn't even crossed his mind that Henry Chapman would be out of town—or that his childhood sanctuary would have been invaded by a crazy faery wearing an oversized US Marine Corps T-shirt.

"Of course I called the cops," she snorted, backing towards the door and rising onto tiptoe to peer through the stained-glass inset. "*I'm* not an idiot. Besides, you could be a serial killer on the run from the FBI, for all I know."

He found himself staring at her, wondering if he'd face-planted into an alternate universe. "I think you've been watching way too much TV."

"I'm a city girl," she replied, reaching out to unlock the door. "We're taught from the cradle to be suspicious of strangers."

The door opened to reveal two cops, who flashed their badges as they stepped into the entrance hall, identifying themselves only as, "Police Department, ma'am."

She waved the flashlight at Ty, her voice a little wobbly as she hit a light switch and continued to address him. "Especially strange men who break into their homes in the middle of the night."

Ignoring her, Ty squinted up at the cops as light flooded the entrance. There was something familiar about the big guy taking in the situation with cool, assessing cop's eyes but he couldn't think past the headache the crazy woman had inflicted on him.

"The question here should be what the penalties are in St John's for illegal squatting," he growled, scowling at the way the bigger cop was now smiling at GI faerie and asking her gently if she was okay, as though he liked what he saw and wouldn't mind getting her number before hauling Ty off to county lockup.

Yeah, right. Like *that* was happening.

He shifted to get to his feet but his vision swam along with his stomach, so he held up his good hand to get someone's attention. Someone who wasn't so damn busy flirting, that was.

"Hey," he growled irritably, when everyone continued to ignore him. "A hand here." They all turned, surprised by his request. Okay, so it was more of a demand, but what the hell? "When you're done flirting, that is," he ended snidely, hiding a smirk at the big cop's hard look—which he returned. The younger guy grinned and GI faerie huffed out a startled laugh.

She went to shove her hair out of her face and nearly conked herself on the head with the flashlight. Ty watched her face flush as she swung away.

"I was… I was… I was just about to call for an ambulance," she ended on a rush, clearly more than a little rattled.

"No!" he yelled, wincing when the sound echoed through his skull and everyone tensed, the cops turning, hands on weapons. He sucked

in a deep breath. "No," he repeated more calmly. "I'm fine."

"You most definitely are not fine," she said decisively, waving the flashlight around again. "Look at you. You're a mess. You need a hospital."

Insulted, he snarled, "I don't need a damn hospital. And will someone take that damn flashlight away before she injures herself?" He waited until she slammed it down on the entrance table and turned to him, hands on her hips and eyes narrowed dangerously.

"Good. Great." He shifted and winced. "I just need a little help, that's all. An explanation would be even better."

"For what?"

"Maybe we'll start with what the hell you're doing in my house and then move on to the unprovoked attack."

"Unprovoked?" she squeaked in outrage. "You looked like the walking dead after my brains. What the heck was I supposed to do?" Three pairs of eyes swung her way and Ty noticed the cops' similar expressions of male confusion. She must have too because she pushed out her lush lower lip, crossed her eyes and huffed out an exasperated breath. "For your information," she continued primly, "this is my house."

"No, it's not." And when no one moved or spoke, "*Dammit*, will someone tell me what the hell is going on?"

She made a tsking sound at his language and turned to the cops. "If he won't go to the hospital, you'll have to hold him down while I do it here." Her voice dropped and she whispered...loudly. "It's going to hurt. We usually strap them to the bed and stick them with a bunch of needles before we try this."

"Hold me—? Needles? Whoa, *you* hold it, lady. Right there." He lifted his good hand in the universal stop gesture and dared them to come any closer. "What do you think you're doing?"

She studied him silently for a couple of seconds before sharing a look with flirty cop. "I'm going to fix your shoulder."

Oh, no. No way in hell.

"No offense, *babe*," he snorted, gritting his teeth against the agony as he struggled to his feet. Where he completely embarrassed himself by swaying as sweat exploded from his pores. His vision swam and it took supreme self-control to stay upright. Fortunately he hadn't eaten since the questionable airline food or he'd be totally humiliating himself. "But I'm not letting a bossy faerie commando anywhere near my shoulder." He jerked his chin behind her. "They can help."

"Oh, for heaven's sake," she snorted, stepping close now that she had two burly cops with guns at her back. "I think the bossy faerie commando is more qualified to do this."

Yeah, right. "I doubt it." He glared at the cop. "Flirty cop here can help me."

"It's Detective Petersen." Flirty cop arched his brows and looked amused but made no move towards him. *Fine.* He turned to the younger cop and got a helpless shrug.

"See," she said smugly. "They know who's in charge here." She patted his shoulder. "But if it makes you feel better, I'll let Detective Petersen help. And don't worry about it," she soothed, as if she was talking to a frightened kid. "I know what I'm doing. You won't feel a thing."

Ty ground his teeth together and sent her a *touch me and die* glare that she totally disregarded by tugging gently but firmly, clearly wanting him back on the floor.

Which was no way in hell happening. He tried

to shrug her off and ended up slapping a hand against the wall when the world spun.

"It'll be much easier this way," she soothed in a soft husky voice that had him blinking and scowling at her again.

"Easier for whom?" he slurred woozily.

Unperturbed, she sent him a smile that was so bright and sweet it distracted him from the crafty gleam in her eyes.

"For you, of course," she murmured, smoothing a hand down his back like he was seven and scared of the dark space under his bed. The move both irritated and pleased him, especially when flirty cop went on hard-eyed alert. Then she added, "This way you won't get any more injuries when you pass out again and crack the floor with your head," and his irritation became outright male insult.

"I am not going to pass…" he began, only to suck in a sharp breath when the world tilted woozily and he slid down the wall to the floor. "Okay…okay, so maybe I do need to, um…lie down."

Clammy and panting, Ty lay on the hard floor, cursing and battling humiliation as the pint-sized tormentor ordered the two cops into position and disappeared upstairs. *Dammit,* this was usually his gig. If word got out he'd never live it down.

Cursing himself for thinking he could just waltz into town and everything would be okay, Ty opened his mouth to order the cops to help him up but she was back with a large towel. "Relax," she soothed. "I can't send you to jail like this."

She slipped the rope towel beneath his back, under his armpit and across his chest. Completely ignoring his gritted curses, she handed the ends to the cops.

Then she planted her knee on his chest and gripped his arm above his cast. Exotic eyes locked with his, she said, "Ready?" and gave it a sharp, hard yank.

Pain exploded through him as his shoulder popped. He let out a ragged groan and lay sweating and groaning while his mini-tormentor sat back on her heels with a loud sigh of relief.

Looking pleased, she gave his chest a comforting rub and rose, affording Ty an unimpeded view of surprisingly long, shapely legs—right up to a pair of teeny boy shorts beneath the baggy T. Boy shorts that were currently hugging world-class curves.

Huh, he thought woozily. Maybe the view from

here wasn't so bad. Then from down a long tunnel he heard her instructing them to take him to the hospital and his pain fog miraculously cleared.

"No," he said firmly, sitting up and hugging his arm to his chest, relieved that the excruciating agony was down to an almost bearable throb. "I told you, no hospital."

"But—"

"No hospital," he all but snarled, and was awarded with a huff of exasperation. "Besides," he slurred, "I'm not leaving you in my dad's house."

No way was he telling anyone that the thought of going into a hospital made him break out in a cold sweat. He couldn't do it. Not yet. Not when his future as a trauma surgeon looked so grim.

CHAPTER TWO

"FINE," PETERSEN SAID TIGHTLY, helping a wobbly Ty onto his feet and all but marching him into the living room. "Let's go. But I warn you, your story had better be good because Dr. Carlyle is here legally. You, not so much."

Ty wanted to shrug off the support but his legs refused to obey the directives from his brain. A lamp was switched on and he blinked in the sudden bright light as he sank down onto the sofa with a groan. Then the man's words registered and he stilled. "Hold it. Who the hell is Dr. Carlyle?"

"I am."

Mini-commando appeared at his side with a huge emergency kit and glass of clear liquid, which she offered. He hoped it was neat vodka and opened his mouth to tell her to just bring the bottle but it emerged instead as a snort of disbelief. "Sure you are," he drawled, taking the glass and saluting her. "Because they let adolescents practice medicine now."

Gold flecks hidden in the swirls of her blue and green eyes flashed, reminding him of sunbursts reflecting off water. It distracted him until he realized that he was letting himself be bewitched by a pair of striking eyes.

Annoyed that it was working, he transferred his attention to the contents of the glass and said tersely, "This is water. Don't you have anything stronger?"

"No. Alcohol exacerbates swelling and internal bleeding." He looked up to tell her that if he had any internal bleeding she was responsible for it, and got caught in her gaze again.

"But I can give you a shot for the pain if you like," she announced, wide-eyed innocence totally belied by the laughter in her eyes.

"Yeah, right," he snorted. Okay, so maybe he'd got ahead of himself there for a moment, but the woman was clearly tougher than she looked. "I have my own meds."

"So," Petersen interrupted, impatient with the delay. "Now that you're all cozy and comfortable, maybe we could see some ID?"

Ty considered telling him what he could do with his request but he was exhausted and knew any argument would just delay their departure.

Collapsing against the back of the sofa, he muttered, "Front pocket."

Neither cop made a move towards him. In fact, they shared a stone-faced look until bossy faerie said, "I'll get it," in a voice that suggested they were all idiots.

He stretched out his leg to give her room and sent Petersen a challenging smirk. He couldn't exactly reach into his pocket with an injured arm and the other holding a glass. Besides, if letting her stick her hand in his pants annoyed flirty cop and got him to leave sooner rather than later, then Ty was game.

But it had been a long time since he'd let a woman reach for anything in his pocket and much to his shock—and stunned bemusement—his body stirred.

What the—?

No way, Ty thought with a sharp sideways look. No way was he attracted to Little Miss Commando. It just wasn't possible.

Was it?

Absolutely not. He didn't like mouthy, bossy women and he didn't like women who attacked defenseless people without provocation.

Her gaze caught his and she flushed, yanking

his wallet out and tossing it at Petersen as though it was a live grenade.

Not meeting anyone's eyes, she grabbed the glass out of his hand and downed the contents before shooting off the couch and bolting behind an armchair as if he was contagious.

Amusement vied with insult. *So*, Ty mused, fascinated by the rosy flush creeping up from the gaping neckline of her T, *she handles an intruder without losing her nerve but sticking her hand in a guy's pocket freaks her out?*

She flashed a glare out the corner of her eye when she caught him staring. Her flush deepened and so did her scowl.

Rubbing a hand over his face, Ty wondered what the heck he was thinking. He'd come to Washington to be alone. Yet here he sat—head pounding like a jackhammer—hugely entertained by his attacker while being interrogated by local cops.

Déjà vu.

Paige slid a sideways glare at the man sprawled on her sofa like he belonged and everyone else were intruders. This was all his fault, she decided huffily. He'd broken into her house, scared her into a new blood group and now he was sitting there looking all impenetrable and imposing, pumping off waves of masculine irritation and blasting testosterone and pheromones around the room like a leaky nuclear reactor.

Silent and deadly.

Especially to unwary females.

Except she was *very* wary. She'd grown up with three older brothers and knew how the alpha mind worked. Innately confident of their place in the world, they silently and arrogantly challenged the rest of humanity. Like her brothers, he seemed to dominate the room completely and effortlessly. As though he wore an invisible sign that said, "Badass territory, enter at own risk."

Curious, she took another peek and caught him still studying her like she was a new species of bug he'd just discovered and wasn't all that impressed by what he saw.

Her face heated and she shifted nervously because she'd caught a glimpse of herself in the foyer mirror and just *had* to look like a wreck the night a hot, rumpled guy broke into her house.

Paige studied him as light from the nearby lamp cast his features in bold relief, highlighting his fierce beauty and illuminating stark blue eyes made bluer by tanned skin.

A shiver snaked through her, promptly tightening her nipples.

What the—?

Paige quickly crossed her arms over her breasts, rubbing her arms as if she was cold. *Stop looking at him,* she ordered herself silently. *He broke into your house and scared you. He is not yummy and he's not harmless.*

No, he wasn't harmless, he was *trouble,* she admitted. The kind of trouble smart women avoided. Fortunately Paige was very smart and could spot trouble at a hundred paces. But even battered and bruised he exuded an almost tangible authority that was pretty darned hard to ignore.

He was one of those seriously hot men—like a Hollywood action hero women sighed over and men secretly wanted to be—with black silky hair tumbling around his lean angular features like a dark halo, highlighting his ice-blue eyes and the unmistakable gleam of intelligence and mockery.

And yet...also unmistakable was a hollow-eyed weariness that made her chest ache. But he wasn't one of her little patients. More like a hot grumpy warrior angel who'd lost his wings in a recent altercation with dark forces and had found himself stranded on earth.

Paige gave a huge mental eye-roll at the fanciful thoughts and ruthlessly ignored the quiver in her belly. Guys with all that seething testosterone usually didn't give her a second glance. Instead, they buzzed around the tall popular girls—girls with long legs and big boobs—like flies around a carcass.

Fortunately the detective turned, interrupting Paige's unwelcome thoughts. He tossed the wallet on the coffee table. "So. What brings a fancy LA doctor to our modest little town?"

Interest caught by his odd tone—kind of confrontational and mocking—she looked at her intruder a little more closely. "LA? Doctor?"

His mouth curled in a slight smirk as he coolly eyed the detective. "Yeah, and I've been sitting here wondering how the hell you became a cop, Petersen."

Petersen's laugh was more of a snort. "Who'd have thought, huh?" He shoved his hands on his hips, jacket open exposing his gun and shield in a blatantly aggressive move. "Your dad know you're here?"

"No. I didn't get a chance to call."

Bemused by the undercurrents in the room, Paige demanded, "Dad?" Her gaze bounced between the three men, hoping to get some clue about what was going on, but they were all wearing their *let's be macho and inscrutable* faces.

"Phone your father and get this sorted fast, Reese," Petersen said, before turning away and heading for the door. "Oh, and welcome home."

"Not arresting me, Detective?" Ty taunted.

The cop paused at the door, his eyes amused as he took in the scene. "Not today. This is your free pass, Reese. Don't make me regret it."

Thoroughly confused and annoyed by the baffling man-speak, Paige demanded again, "What? What did I miss? Who is he? And, *dammit*, why are you leaving?"

Petersen gave a huge sigh and shook his head. "Ask him."

"What? *No*," Paige said, jumping to her feet. "You can't just leave him here. What am I supposed to do with him? Take him away."

"He's harmless," the cop said with faint mockery. "And it really is his house."

And before Paige could do more than stutter, "B-but," the detectives had disappeared down the passage. Through the roaring in her ears she heard the front door closing behind them.

For several long seconds she stood staring open-mouthed at the doorway, before turning and demanding, "What was that?"

"Nothing," "fancy doc" sighed, rubbing a large hand over his face. "Ancient history. But he's right, I'm harmless." And when she opened her mouth to laugh at that big whopper, he drawled, "Believe me, doing anything more strenuous than breathing is currently beyond my capabilities." He shifted then winced. "I just need a drink and a place to crash. The rest can wait till morning."

Realizing she was still clutching the emergency kit like her life depended on it, Paige set it down on the coffee table with a little more force than necessary.

"No."

She didn't quite know what she was saying no to, the alcohol, him spending the rest of the night in her house or the fact that her life was spinning out of control...*and just when she'd thought she was finally getting it together.*

"No?"

She caught his expression and nearly laughed at the stunned disbelief on his face. As though people—women most probably—didn't say no to him very often. She gave a silent snort. They probably didn't. Not looking the way he did—all simmering male irritation and dark angel looks. Women probably lined up hoping to tease a smile from that mouth...or something that required mouth-to-mouth resuscitation.

Her spine snapped straight. Well, not *this* woman. She could resus herself just fine, thank you. And all those yummy pheromones flying around like busy little bees looking for the nearest flower to pollinate could...could...well, they could just buzz off.

There would be *no* pollinating.

Not this flower. Nuh-uh. No way.

Not that he looked like he wanted to pollinate her flower, she admitted with brutal honesty. He'd called her an adolescent and a bossy faerie commando—which put a *big* black mark against him as far as she was concerned. He was just like every other alpha guy who thought they were in charge and everyone—women especially—was eager to obey.

"No," she repeated more firmly. "No alcohol." *Right. Let's go with that one.* "And no crashing on the couch until you tell me who you are and why you broke into my house. You can do that while I strap your shoulder. Besides, I know the owner and you are definitely *not* him."

He sighed and rubbed his forehead like *she* was giving *him* a headache when the opposite was actually true.

"Look," he said wearily, "I'm fine. I don't need doctoring. And before you get all bent out of shape," he continued curtly when she opened her mouth to argue, "I can handle my own damn injuries." His ice-blue eyes took a lazy trip from the top of her head to her bare toes. "And as appealing as you are..." his mouth curled up at one corner as though her appearance amused him "... I just want to be alone. I really, *really* need that." He closed his eyes. "So...can you wave your magic faerie wand and disappear?"

"Ha-ha, very funny," she snapped. "If you think I'm about to head off to bed with a stranger on my couch, you can think again."

The look he sent her most probably sent people running for cover. Paige, who had weathered scarier looks and survived, returned it coolly.

Finally he muttered something that sounded like, "Bossy little smartass," and gestured to the emergency kit. "Fine," he said wearily. "Just get a move on so we can both get some sleep before the night is completely shot. And there's my ID." He jerked his chin at his wallet on the coffee table.

"Knock yourself out. Call Dr. Henry Chapman too if it'll make you feel better. I might not have seen him in a while but I'm pretty sure he still remembers he has a son."

Paige was halfway down the stairs the next morning when she caught sight of her flashlight on the entrance table and remembered her boss and landlord's grumpy son on her sofa. Or, as she'd dubbed him—after he'd grunted and promptly thrown an arm across his eyes after she'd strapped his shoulder, in a blatant message for her to get lost—Dr. Bad Attitude.

Feeling like a thief in her own house, she tiptoed to the living room and peered around the door to find him still sprawled across her sofa where she'd left him. One long leg hung over the end, the other was foot-planted on the floor, probably to keep him from rolling off the sofa.

The blankets and pillow were halfway across the room as though he'd flung them there in a fit of temper.

The breath she hadn't been aware she was holding escaped in a silent whoosh. So…she hadn't dreamed him up. Neither had she dreamed up what a very fine specimen of manhood he was, she admitted with dismay.

But she didn't need this kind of complication, she told herself firmly. Boss's son or not, she'd send him on his way the instant he opened his sexy blue eyes.

Catching herself drooling at the sight of all that taut tanned skin highlighted by neon pink taping, Paige tried schooling her features into a frown. It didn't work, especially when she recalled his reaction at her liberal application of pink. Instead of making him look ridiculously feminine—which was what she'd intended—all it had done was emphasize his dark smoldering masculinity.

Covering her mouth to stifle her snickers, Paige yawned and retreated to the kitchen. She needed a hefty dose of caffeine if she was going to get him out of her house.

She filled the reservoir and measured out ground coffee then pressed the start button and was in the middle of a jaw-cracking yawn when she heard ringing. The sound galvanized her into action and she shot out of the kitchen, following the sound because she couldn't remember where she'd left her phone.

Muttering frantically, she prayed the ringing

would stop before it woke the grizzly camped on her—

"Oops," she said breathlessly, rushing into the living room to find the bear, wearing low-slung jeans, a mile of pink tape and a black scowl, with her shoulder bag in his hand, dumping the contents on the coffee table.

"Hey," she said when he shoved everything out, presumably looking for her cellphone. When he found it he stabbed at the screen with a long tanned finger, heaving a huge sigh as it went silent.

"Hey," she said again, rushing forward to snatch up her phone, glaring at him when she saw that he'd ended the call. But he'd already resumed a horizontal position with one arm slung across his eyes and all she could see of his face was a very nicely sculpted, very grim mouth and a hard jaw covered in a few days' growth.

Her own black scowl was completely wasted. "That could have been an emergency."

He grunted in what he probably thought was a very eloquent reply before adding, "Since when is 'kick-ass grl' an emergency?" in a deep rough voice that might have sent shivers up her spine if she hadn't been annoyed.

"Maybe that's what I call my boss," she shot back heatedly, because she'd totally felt the shivers, darn it. When a ping came from her phone, she stabbed the screen bad-temperedly to access the message.

Hrd abt lst nite. Sid's in 15. I'm buying.

She didn't question how "kick-ass grl" knew about her midnight visitor. St John's wasn't *that* big and everyone—especially emergency personnel—seemed to know everything that happened within minutes of it happening.

Frankie Bryce was an EMT and seemed to know stuff before it happened. Probably because she had friends in high and not-so-high places.

But it'd been a long week and Paige wasn't about to turn down free breakfast, especially at Sid's, which was a hugely popular diner on the boardwalk. It overlooked the harbor where the coastguard did their water training—in skin-tight wetsuits and sometimes jammers—and served the best coffee and pie in town.

That she'd have to cough up details of last night was a given but Frankie had grown up in Port St. John's and might know about Tyler Reese, hot and grumpy son of Port St. John's favorite doctor, and fancy LA doctor of who knew what?

She thumbed a quick reply then bent to scoop up all the purse junk Dr. Cranky had exploded all over the coffee table, turning her head in time to see him eyeing her butt. She squeaked out a protest and straightened so fast she almost gave herself whiplash.

"Hey," she accused, slapping her hands over her bottom. "Eyes off, Mr. Cranky, or I might decide not to offer you any coffee before I toss you out."

Ty snorted, unconcerned that he'd been caught ogling her posterior. "You had your shot." He yawned, eyes as gritty as his temper. "The next one's mine."

She stomped off muttering about rude unwelcome guests and Ty waited until he was alone before pushing to his feet. He followed the smell of coffee to the kitchen, feeling like he'd been run over by a train.

A train named Paige Carlyle, he thought darkly.

He'd already inhaled one mug and was reaching for his second when she bolted down the stairs, looking flustered and sexy in a bright blue tank top tucked into faded jeans. The outfit hugged her sweet curves and clung to surprisingly long, shapely legs.

Dragging his gaze away from her legs was difficult but he managed, noting absently that her wild hair had been tamed into a shiny inky bob that swung against her delicate jaw. Feathery bangs framed her exotic face, making her eyes appear bigger this morning—if that was possible.

She stopped short when she saw him, no doubt because he was staring at her like she'd just popped through a tear in the space-time continuum. But what was he to do? The transformation from wild faerie commando to...to girl-next-door was startling.

"What?" she demanded, looking down at herself, probably to check for missing fabric, a streak of toothpaste...or a big neon sign that said, "Bite me." Apparently finding nothing amiss, she looked up and with her arms out at her sides in a *what's wrong with my appearance?* gesture she asked, "What?" again, this time with annoyance.

Alarmed to find his tongue stuck to the roof of his mouth, Ty just shook his head. No way was he telling her that she looked good enough to eat and that he suddenly couldn't remember his last meal. Turning away, he poured himself more coffee and decided that Dr. Paige Carlyle was too fresh and sweet, too vulnerable for someone as cynical as him.

She'd probably grown up loved and indulged by her family while he...well, needless to say he didn't believe in love or happily-ever-after. His mother regarded her two children with cool disinterest, unless they disappointed her then it was with cold displeasure; and his father with absentminded affection. He'd seen Henry Chapman look at his dog that way too.

Better that she think he was rude and obnoxious.

Besides, she was hardly his type anyway. He dated tall sophisticated women; women who knew the score and weren't interested in anything more than dinner and a good time. He was fairly sure Little Miss Medic hadn't even heard there *was* a score. And with *that* mouth, she certainly wouldn't be easy to ignore.

Okay, so the rest of her wasn't easy to ignore either but he was pretty sure it was because she reminded him of a creature from some graphic novel fantasy world.

She appeared in the doorway, wearing a little jacket, shoulder bag slung casually over her shoulder. "You're still here," she said, nibbling on her soft lip and looking adorably self-conscious.

Instead of answering, he lifted the mug in a silent toast, spooked by the abrupt desire to yank her against him and taste her shiny pink mouth. In fact, if she didn't leave soon he might do just that and forgo mainlining caffeine altogether. It would go a long way to waking him up.

"Anyway…" she continued in a way that made Ty think she was rolling her eyes in her head. "I was thinking." She bit her lip uncertainly. "About what Detective Petersen said last night?" He arched his brow, wondering where she was going with this. "Anyway," she sighed impatiently, "I wondered why you came here instead of going to your father's house."

Ah. His mouth twisted wryly as he studied her over the rim of his coffee mug. The last thing he wanted was to discuss his almost non-existent relationship with his father…but…then again he supposed he did owe her an explanation.

"My grandparents built this house. It's where my father grew up and where I spent every summer until I was eighteen." She tilted her head and confusion marred the smooth skin of her forehead.

He sighed. "I would have called my father but

my phone died and I thought I'd surprise him. But don't worry, I'll be out of your hair as soon as this caffeine kicks in."

She was silent a long moment before giving a short nod. "Do you need help...um...dressing?"

Immediately an image of her helping him *un*dress flashed into his mind and before he could stop it, his mouth curved. Seeing it, she rolled her eyes and went bright pink.

"You are such a...a *guy*," she accused, turning away. "I have to get going. And since you're my boss's son, I'm not going to throw you out or call the cops. But I *am* going to assume you'll be gone by the time I get back."

He moved to the archway to watch her open the front door. "Lock up behind you," she tossed over her shoulder and closed the door with an almost slam.

He found himself smiling for no reason other than he'd managed to get under her skin and lifted the mug in a cocky salute to the fact that he finally had what he wanted—blessed silence.

He enjoyed it for a few moments until his amusement faded. Turning, he rinsed out his mug and placed it in the dishwasher. Somehow all the air, all the life had been sucked out with her departure. It had never happened before—with *anyone*—which meant he needed to get out of there before she returned.

Before he was tempted to help *her* undress and find out if she was a figment of his overactive imagination or the real deal.

CHAPTER THREE

PAIGE HEADED FOR SID'S, telling herself that she was giving Dr. Bad Attitude exactly what he wanted—space. But the truth was she'd been grateful for the excuse to escape.

It was unnerving to have a man in her living space—especially one who made her want to growl and sigh at the same time. Who made her tingle in places that hadn't tingled in far too long one minute, and stifle the urge to throw something at him the next.

She didn't like it. Not one little bit. She'd learned early on that guys like him weren't attracted to women like her. She was the eternal "cute girl" they treated like a little sister.

Wanting something—or someone—she couldn't have reminded her too much of a past she'd thought she'd long outgrown.

She'd had everything until her mother had died. She lost both parents that day, her mother to ovarian cancer and her father to grief. He'd retreated into his work, leaving a devastated pre-teen to cope with her grief alone because her brothers were much older and didn't do girly things like talk about their feelings.

As if grieving for the loss of the most important person in all their lives was somehow unmanly.

She'd tried and failed to keep the family together, as she'd promised her mom. One by one her brothers had left, Bryn, the oldest, to accept a position as assistant manager of a football team in San Diego, Eric for the SEALs program, and Quinn to the US Air Force, where he flew classified aircraft on top-secret missions.

Then her father had unexpectedly remarried and it had been like losing everything all over again. Her brothers had rarely visited and she'd suddenly felt like an unwanted reminder of her father's pain.

To be honest, he hadn't known what to do with her and he'd probably thought a new mother and step-siblings would help her cope with grief. But they hadn't, and instead she'd retreated into her school work.

In her senior year salvation had come in the form of a full bursary to med school and everyone had seemed to heave a huge sigh of relief. With

Paige gone there had been no need for her father to feel guilty every time he saw her.

She'd thought that by acing her exams she would get his approval, but despite finishing her degree early and at the top of her class, her father hadn't even attended her graduation. Instead, he'd sent a gift and a note with his apologies that the family would be in Aruba.

Dammit, she'd always wanted to go to Aruba.

At least her three brothers had made it—Eric in fatigues on his way home from a mission and Quinn in full US Air Force uniform. They'd made her laugh with their antics and she'd scarcely felt her father's absence.

Fine. She'd been devastated but she'd finally acknowledged that she was on her own. Her brothers had their own busy lives and their father…well, she could totally take care of herself.

Besides, it was safer not to let people close. It hurt too much when they left.

Francis Abigail Bryce was already in their booth, looking like a movie star in her dark blue paramedic jumpsuit. She'd ordered coffee and was sitting there with a faraway expression on her face. And because she looked just a little bit sad, Paige said the first thing that came to her mind as she slid into the booth opposite her.

"You do know that redheads are supposed to have freckles, don't you?"

"And did *you* know that people who've beaten up late-night intruders with their awesome ninja skills aren't supposed to look so fresh and perky the next day?" Frankie answered smartly, eyeing Paige with sharp green eyes. "Why do you?"

Paige grimaced. "You heard, huh?"

"That's like saying have I heard the coastguard is in town," Frankie snorted, and slid a latte across the table. "I was on duty last night when your call came through. If I hadn't had an emergency I would have helped you bury the body."

Paige grinned and lifted her latte in a toast. "You're the best friend ever. But..." She paused to take a huge gulp, sighing in pleasure when the hot creamy liquid hit her stomach. "As it turned out, he wasn't dead, just concussed. But breakfast first, I'm starving," she said as the waitress approached.

Once the waitress left with their order, Frankie demanded a minute-by-minute account of her midnight adventure, laughing when Paige recounted Ty calling her a bossy little smartass and a faerie commando, and snorting indelicately at his manly reaction to pink tape.

"Men are idiots," Frankie said dryly, "including Ty Reese, so don't go getting any idiotic ideas about saving him."

Paige rolled her eyes and waited as the waitress delivered their food. Tyler Reese needed saving about as much as a prowling mountain lion. But that didn't mean she wasn't curious about him.

Trying for casually offhand, she said, "So...you do know him?"

"Hmm," Frankie murmured, looking amused.

"And?" Paige prompted a little impatiently, when her friend took another bite of omelet without replying. "Spill already before I hurt you."

Frankie nearly choked. "Like you could," she snorted, wiping her mouth with the napkin Paige shoved at her. "Ty's right. With those huge exotic eyes and delicate face, you do look like a faerie. If you weren't my best friend, I'd hate you."

Paige snorted, "Yeah, right," because Frankie was one of those exotically beautiful redheads. Smooth creamy skin, thick lustrous hair *and*...and *darn*...she looked a million dollars in a swimsuit.

"So...what do you know about him?"

Frankie studied Paige for a moment. "You mean

other than he has a thing for stacked blonde Malibu beach babes?"

"Yeah." Paige sighed, wondering at the rush of intense disappointment at the news. It was a ridiculous reaction to have about a guy who'd broken into her house and scared the heck out of her. Besides, guys like Tyler Reese had genetically built-in radar for beautiful blondes—or redheads—and having grown up with three brothers who'd dated endless lines of stacked blonde bombshells, it was something she thought she'd accepted.

"Other than that. Which is hardly breaking news, by the way. Guys *always* go for the hot blondes."

Frankie sighed and said again, "Men are idiots," and looked miserable, but after a couple of beats she seemed to shake off her strange mood. "He's not for you."

That brought Paige up short. Her breakfast abruptly turned to lead in her stomach. "Not that I'm interested or anything," she said shoving her plate aside, "but what's wrong with me?"

"It's not you, it's him." Frankie broke off and studied Paige silently before saying, "Okay, maybe it is you."

Paige didn't know why the idea that Frankie

thought she wasn't good enough for Tyler Reese hurt so much. She should be used to being ignored, not pretty, sexy or popular enough, but the truth was, it would be nice to be a kick-ass girl they drooled over. Like Frankie—movie-star beautiful and built like an underwear model, only with attitude.

A *lot* of attitude.

"Oh, don't look at me like that, honey. I only meant that you're too open and generous for someone whose mother is the Wicked Ice Witch of the West. Believe me," she continued when Paige opened her mouth to deny that she was interested in Ty Reese, "I've known him my whole life. At one time he, Nate and Jack were inseparable. They did *everything* together. Including try their stupid moves on everything with breasts. No, jeez," she snorted. "Even *before* girls got breasts they were stealing kisses and breaking hearts." She shook her head. "You don't want to go there." After a moment's silence she said vehemently, "It'd be like stuffing your heart in a mincer and turning it on grind. You don't deserve that. No one deserves that."

Paige knew Frankie's brother Jack had been an army ranger before being KIA a few years ago.

She opened her mouth to ask about Nate but was distracted by the odd expression on Frankie's face. Concerned, she turned and followed her gaze in time to see three guys entering the diner. They were dressed in US coastguard uniforms and the hotness factor was enough to raise the temperature in the diner by a thousand degrees.

"Who's that?" she asked curiously, when Frankie made a little sound of distress. She looked stunned. Kind of like she'd run into a wall.

"Huh?"

Paige jerked her chin at the newcomers. "Who's that?"

Her friend took a deep breath, looking strangely flushed and panicked. "No one," she muttered, lurching abruptly out of the booth. "Look, I gotta go. I'm teaching a first-aid class in twenty minutes."

This was news to Paige. "I thought you were off duty for the next few days." But because Frankie looked so rattled—a look Paige had never seen on her before—she didn't pursue her sudden suspicion that Frankie knew at least one of the coasties.

Or was maybe running scared?

"JT bailed from the senior center program at the last minute so I said I'd take it. Don't worry," she said, when Paige opened her mouth to remind her of their plans. "I haven't forgotten our hiking trip. Meet you at twelve?"

Paige nodded, her fascinated gaze moving beyond Frankie to the tallest and hottest of the trio and... *Oh, wow...* Her eyes widened. The tall dangerous coastie...he must be the one her friend was running from because the guy was staring their way, and the abrupt tension emanating from Frankie told Paige there was definite history there.

She must have made a sound because Frankie's eyes widened and she looked spooked—like she wanted to bolt but was forcing herself to act cool.

"I really have to go," Frankie said abruptly. "But a word of advice here. Stay away from those guys, Paige. They're bad news. In fact, stay away from the whole male gender. They suck."

And with that she spun on her heel and headed for the door.

Fascinated, Paige watched the tall, hot coastie looking granite-faced and dangerous as he contemplated her friend's stiff departing back.

That's one hot BAB, she thought, referring to her and Frankie's name for bad alpha boys. Or was that badass boys? She couldn't remember because they'd both been a little tipsy at the time.

She could feel the simmering testosterone and attitude from clear across the room. Then he turned and their eyes met. *Yikes,* she thought, *a very bad BAB.* And, boy, he had "military" badass written all over him.

Used to dealing with alpha males, Paige narrowed her eyes and mouthed a fierce "I'm watching you", feeling invincible because just last night she had taken out an intruder with nothing but a flashlight and her awesome ninja skills.

After a long moment his mouth kicked up at one corner like he found her cute and amusing, and right there, in Sid's Diner, Paige decided Frankie was right.

Men sucked and Paige was going to have no problem heeding her own as well as Frankie's advice.

She was going to stay away from men—especially the tall dark cranky ones who broke into people's houses as easily as they broke women's hearts.

Ty was trying to dry himself one-handed after a shower when he heard pounding on the front door. Wondering if some of the crazy women he'd left LA to escape had tracked him down, he wrapped a towel around his hips and whipped open the bathroom door…coming face to face with—

"Aaaai-ya!"

He ducked just in time to avoid being beaned with a…frying pan?

Reacting without thinking, he shot out a hand and yanked the pan away before Paige Carlyle could take another swing at him.

"What the hell, woman?"

She let rip with an ear-piercing shriek and scrambled backwards, her expression one of shocked surprise. Before Ty could reassure her that he wasn't a pervert hiding in her shower, the front door crashed open and heavy steps pounded up the stairs.

A large man appeared at the top of the landing in a fighter's crouch, dark eyes hard and cold, ready to take down the enemy. In that instant Ty's towel lost the battle and slid to the floor.

The newcomer instantly took in the scene and after a stunned pause visibly relaxed. His mouth kicked up at one corner as he rose to his full height.

"Well, now," he drawled, hooking the arm of his aviator shades in the neck of his tee-shirt. "Am I missing something, T?"

Ty didn't know who was more surprised by the frozen tableau on the landing, him, Paige or—

"Nate?"

Slapping a hand to her chest, Paige gasped furiously, "*Omigod!* What are you *doing* here?" and collapsed against the banister. She wrapped one arm around the landing rail as though to keep her from sliding to the floor. "I thought you'd left," she squeaked, her tone rising into the stratosphere. "I thought you'd... Who is *he*?" She gestured wildly at Nate, nearly whacking herself in the head. "And what the heck is a m-military B-BAB doing in my h-house?"

He and Nathan Oliver—whom Ty had last seen just before he'd deployed to some hotspot six months ago—shared a confused look. "Military BAB?" Ty asked what was on both their minds.

She finally lost her battle with gravity and plopped onto the floor, breathing as though she'd run up the north face of the Olympic Mountains. "I'm still asleep, aren't I?" she gasped, rubbing the heel of her hand against her chest and clearly on the verge of a coronary. Then she looked up and locked eyes with the part of him at eye level and gave a strangled squeak.

"Omigod!" she gasped, slapping a hand over her eyes. "My eyes."

Nate snickered as Ty whipped the frying pan up to cover himself. He sent his friend a dark look and turned to apologize but Paige had drawn up her legs and dropped her forehead on her knees. She was breathing heavily and muttering to herself.

"This is just a nightmare, Paige," he heard her mutter in a singsong voice. "Wake up and take a *deep* breath." She made a few gasping sounds. "That's it...nice and easy." For several long moments she continued to breathe like she was practicing for the labor ward while he and Nate watched in fascination.

Finally... "There you are. Now you're going to open your eyes and *everything* will be back to normal. Nice...and...normal." Another deep breath, this one less panicked. "No more sexy... *naked*...men." She gave a snorting laugh that he was pretty sure was an insult to his manhood. "Or military BABs anywhere. *Poof.* Gone."

Ty grimaced and bent to scoop up the towel, managing to wrap it clumsily around his waist before Paige looked up.

"You're still here," she accused, taking in the

towel clutched at his hips before cutting her eyes
to Nate. Arms folded across his chest and leaning
casually against the wall, he studied them with
a casualness belied by his watchful eyes. "Why
are you still here?"

Ty wasn't sure if she was talking to him or Nate
and opened his mouth to apologize but, "You
think I'm sexy?" slipped out instead.

Nate snorted rudely and Paige rolled her eyes.
"Please. You've clearly let yourself go," she said
breathlessly, her gaze cutting to his towel and then
sliding away. "You're a mess."

Not likely, he thought when Nate laughed with
the appreciation of a long-time friend. "You said
sexy naked men. And as I'm the only *naked* one
here—"

"Don't mind him, sweetheart," Nate interrupted
dryly. "He's always been shy about letting girls
see him naked." He pushed away from the wall
and pulled Paige to her feet. "Hi," he said. "I'm
Nate and you must be the cute doctor that took
down a dangerous intruder one-handed."

"It was dark," Ty growled, wiping water out of
his eyes on his equally damp shoulder. "Don't
mind me," he muttered when Paige allowed her-

self to be steered towards the stairs. "I'll be down as soon as I get dressed."

"Take your time," Nate called over his shoulder. "Dr. Cutie and I are going to get better acquainted."

After a couple of beats Ty turned and returned to the bathroom. By the time he descended the stairs, Nate was shoulder-propped against the arch leading into the kitchen, sipping coffee.

"Still spreading joy and happiness everywhere you go, I see," his friend drawled laconically.

"And you're still trying—and failing, I might add—to look like the coolest kid on the block."

Nathan Oliver chuckled. "I don't have to try any more, T, it just comes naturally. You, on the other hand, look like sh—"

"Yeah, yeah," he interrupted, catching Paige's quick furtive sideways look and the faint flush staining her cheeks. "I know exactly how I look."

"I heard you got beaten up by a girl and just had to see for myself." He chuckled at the exasperated sound Paige made in the back of her throat and reached out to ruffle her hair. "Did a good job on him too."

Ty's eyes cut to Paige, wondering at the casual way his friend had touched her. "I already looked like this before a crazy person jumped me and tried to beat me up with a flashlight."

She heaved a huge sigh and Ty could almost hear her eyes roll around in her head. He moved into the kitchen and purposely crowded her as he went for the coffeepot, biting back a smile when she sucked in a sharp breath and scuttled out of his way, muttering what sounded like, "He's just a stupid BAB, Paige. Get a grip."

"What's a bab?" he asked, after pouring coffee for himself and leaning against the counter. He eyed her over the mug rim and tried not to notice the silky smoothness of her skin.

She started, like he'd caught her doing something indecent. "BAB?"

A frown slowly wrinkled the smooth skin of her forehead and Ty had to restrain himself from reaching out and smoothing it with his thumb. *What the hell?* He wasn't a touchy-feely kind of guy so why the hell did he suddenly want to touch her?

Again refusing to meet his eyes, she muttered something beneath her breath and he had to dip his head to peer into her flushed face.

"What's that, Dr. Cutie? You say something?"

"No." She shoved her way past him. "Excuse

me," she said with excruciating politeness, and headed for the stairs, muttering, "And the next person to call me that is dead meat."

"Where are you going?" he asked, watching her take the stairs at a mad dash. He heard her say, "Out," as she disappeared. Thoroughly confused, he turned to Nate. "What the hell did you say to upset her?"

"Me?" Nate drawled. "I didn't do a thing but rush to rescue the damsel in distress. You, on the other hand, were the creepy stalker standing there dressed in nothing but pink tape, and…" he leaned forward and sniffed "…smelling like a spring garden." He chuckled and flashed a look up the stairs where Paige had disappeared. "Maybe I should invite her sailing. Cute and feisty is an irresistible combination."

"And maybe you should back off," Ty growled, feeling unaccountably annoyed. "What are you, seventeen? She's not the kind of woman you take sailing just because you need to get laid. Pick someone who knows the score."

"Oh, yeah?" Nate drawled. "And how would you know? I thought you two only met last night."

"We did," Ty growled. "When she tried to crack my skull open."

"Then what's your prob—? Ah." Nate nodded sagely. "I get it. You want her for yourself."

"What—? Of course not," Ty scoffed, feeling his gut clench. "She's a bossy pain in the ass who decorated me in pink, for God's sake." He jerked his chin at his cast. "I'm here because I need peace and quiet to think about what I'll do if I can't do surgery again. I don't need an annoying distraction, no matter how cute and feisty. Besides, she's not *my* type any more than she's *yours*."

"Oh, I don't know," Nate said, thoughtfully. "I think cute and feisty would be a refreshing change, don't you?"

"No, I don't. It would be suicidal."

Behind them they heard a sound and turned to see Paige standing at the bottom of the stairs looking like she was considering which of them to maim first.

"Oh, hey," Ty said. "I was just—"

"I'm leaving," she interrupted. "I hope your visit with your father goes well. I left his address on the entrance table. Please lock up when you leave." Her tone, as cool as her expression, suggested she hoped it was soon.

She'd obviously heard.

"Listen, I didn't mean—" he began, but the

front door slammed. Hard. He winced. "I think she heard."

"Yep." Nate clamped a hand on Ty's shoulder in brotherly support. "And now you're scum just like the rest of us. Welcome to the club."

CHAPTER FOUR

A FEW DAYS LATER, Paige was still smarting over the fact that Tyler Reese thought she was an annoying distraction he didn't want. She told herself she didn't care that "cute and feisty" wasn't his type because snarly and arrogant certainly wasn't hers.

She still shuddered because, as far as she was concerned, cute was a metaphor for "fun but too ugly to date" or "you're like a sister to me". She wouldn't go there if her hair was on fire and he held the only glass of water left in the universe.

Fortunately, by the time she and Frankie had returned from their hike, her house was empty except for a thank-you note taped to the refrigerator. It had obviously been scrawled by Nate.

Dear Paige,
T says he's sorry for being a bonehead and flashing the family jewels—but you've probably already forgotten that. He also wanted

to thank you for your hospitality and for not insisting he be incarcerated like a common criminal. He has a thing about jail in this town. Anyway I'd like to thank you for knocking some sense into his thick skull—although it might take time to sink in.

Nate.

P.S. I was serious about taking you sailing.

Right. Like she would actually accept. She was fairly certain it had just been to get a reaction out of Ty. *Why* was something she tortured herself with along with other thoughts of him. Thoughts like, if he'd returned to California. Like if he and Henry Chapman were getting along.

Like if she'd exaggerated his "endowments" in her own mind.

She told herself she had because no one looked that good without being "enhanced" by a photo editor.

But she couldn't stop thinking about something else she'd overheard him say to his friend. Something that explained why he was so grumpy. He was a surgeon who'd injured his dominant hand. She wondered what had happened and had questioned Frankie about it, but her friend didn't know either.

It was six-thirty and the chilly morning wind blowing right off the straits caught Paige when she left the house. She considered going back for a jacket but it was a twenty-minute drive through town on a quiet day and she didn't want to be late for the morning briefing.

Her aged sedan, Old Bertha, sat hunched against the curb looking both familiar and forlorn. Paige gave the roof an affectionate pat and quickly unlocked the door so she could escape the wind. Over the past week they'd had gloriously fine weather and the icy gusts coming off the straits were an unwelcome reminder of the Pacific North West's reputation for unpredictable weather—especially this time of year.

She dumped her shoulder bag on the seat beside her and shoved the key into the ignition. Instead of the engine turning over, all she got was an ominous click.

Used to her car's eccentricities, Paige said a silent prayer and tried again. Nothing.

"No, no, *no!*" she begged, heart skipping a beat as she flicked a glance at the dash clock and calculated the time she had to fiddle with the engine.

"Just this once, girl. *Please*." Bracing herself, she silently urged the car to start, then sucked in a breath, mentally crossed all her fingers *and* toes, and turned the key.

And got a whole lot of...nothing. *Dammit.*

Muttering under her breath, she popped the hood and shoved open the door, grabbing her phone so she could call the hospital. Frankie would also be heading to work soon and could swing by.

Hopefully.

She heaved up the hood and propped it up with the metal thingy, shivering as icy wind sneaked cold fingers down the back of her neck into her snug long-sleeved T.

Having absolutely no idea what she was looking for, she shoved her head under the hood, hoping the problem—like a loose wire or something—would jump out at her.

"Well, Paige," she muttered irritably, "maybe you should have taken motor mechanics at school instead of calculus. Is calculus going to help you fix Bertha? No, and neither is—"

"Problem?"

With a startled squeak, she jerked upright and whacked her head smartly on the hood. For a couple of seconds she saw stars before impatient masculine hands pulled her free.

"What the hell, woman?" Tyler Reese growled in that deep bedroom voice that sent shivers right up her spine only to have them spreading further. Like *everywhere.*

Or maybe it was the heat of his hands on her as he gently probed her head because her body responded—embarrassingly fast.

Her nipples tightened—but that could easily be from the cold—and her knees wobbled. She finally gathered her wits enough to shove at the broad chest blocking her view so she could rub her own damn head. And breathe without getting a lung full of warm masculine scent that made her want to bury her face in his throat.

Oh, boy. Not good.

Lurching out of range, she scowled up at him. "Ouch, *dammit.* What are you doing, sneaking up on me?" she demanded irritably, because he clearly wasn't feeling "it" like she was. Then, realizing he was outside her house—*what the heck?*—she gulped. Her eyes widened. "Are you stalking me?"

One brow rose arrogantly. He said mildly, "Good morning to you too, Dr. Carlyle." And when she just scowled at him, he sighed. "Okay, not a morning person. Good to know and to answer your question; no, I am not stalking you. I saw you pop the hood and pretend you know what you're doing."

"I am too a morning person," she practically snarled. "And how do you know I don't know what I'm doing? Maybe I took a class in motor mechanics."

His eyebrow rose up his forehead in patent disbelief. "You took calculus instead."

"Yes," she sighed. "And even if I did, Bertha is selective about who works on her." She pulled her phone out and began thumbing through her contacts.

"Bertha?"

"Car," she said absently, tapping out an urgent message to the dayshift ER supervisor. By the time she looked up, Ty had stuck his head under the hood and was fiddling around one handed, muttering about "idiots who don't take care of their cars".

Ignoring his comments—because she was still mad at him—she joined him, hoping he knew what he was doing and would magically get Bertha started. Instead she was assailed by his warm masculine scent.

Damn. She sent him a sideways glance that was filled with rebuke. It should be illegal for a man to smell so good and—despite the fading bruises—*look* so good.

"What?" he asked, attention firmly on some alien engine part she didn't recognize. Busy resenting the hell out of him, she said the first thing that popped into her head.

"Huh?"

"You're staring at me," he said mildly.

"I was just wondering if I was having nightmares about zombie psychos or if you're really standing here, messing with me...uh, with my engine, I mean. My car," she said huffily, when his mouth curled. "Messing with my car."

Instead of answering, his head turned and suddenly his face was an inch from hers. Their gazes locked and for a breathless moment she felt herself sink under his powerful sexual spell, wondering at the heavy liquid sensations taking over her limbs...and the wild kamikaze butterflies dive-bombing her belly.

A little voice in the back of her mind yelled,

Move away from the sexy BAB, Paige. He's trouble, remember.

"Paige."

She blinked slowly, fighting the pull of him, thinking, *This is bad. This is really, really bad.*

"What's bad?" he asked, and it was a couple of beats before she realized she'd spoken out loud. Pressing her lips together, she shook her head, recalling that he'd already called her a crazy person.

"I'm sorry," he said, the quiet intensity in his gaze echoed in his tone.

Her forehead tightened in confusion. "Sorry?"

"About what you overheard the other day. I didn't mean…well, it."

"Huh." Paige stepped back from the car on wobbly legs and leaned her hip against the fender. She folded her arms beneath her breasts. His eyes dropped from her mouth and, to her horror, her nipples promptly tightened. His mouth curved and she was tempted to punch him because she wasn't one of those voluptuous beach babes he probably dated in droves.

His gaze rose up her neck, past her chin to linger on her mouth before meeting hers. The laser heat in them had her knees wobbling.

No, darn it. No wobbling. You're mad at him, remember.

"Didn't mean for me to hear, you mean?" she drawled coolly.

"No," he said, shaking his head. "I didn't mean it."

"It?" she enquired politely, gritting her teeth against the melting heat taking up residence in her body beneath that hooded gaze. "What exactly are you sorry for? The part where you called me a bossy pain in the ass and an annoying distraction you didn't need or want? Or was it the part that dating me 'would be awful, not to mention suicidal'?"

He sighed and shoved a hand through his hair as though she was being deliberately difficult. "The latter," he explained with more than a hint of exasperation. "Definitely the latter because you're still an annoying, bossy pain in the ass."

And just when she was about to tell him that he needn't worry about her wanting to date him even if he was the very last man in the freaking universe, from directly behind them a gruff voice asked, "Problem?" nearly giving her a coronary.

She spun around with a startled gasp, forgetting that she was perched against the left headlight, and would have fallen into the road if Ty hadn't reached out and yanked her back onto her feet. She immediately growled at him and pulled away, blinking at her neighbor who stood watching them with amused curiosity.

Harry Andersen had been a coastguard for fifty years and now spent his time watering his plants, looking out for Paige, helping the neighborhood seniors and keeping an ear on his ham radio and an eye on the weather. He claimed his bones were better barometers for weather changes than any new-fangled instruments the coastguards used.

In the months she'd been here, Paige had grown to love the old man. His face had that lived-in quality of someone who'd spent years squinting into the sun and wind that came off the ocean.

His wise brown eyes were often a little bleak and lonely because his wife of fifty years had passed away a year before Paige's arrival in Port St. John's.

"Hi, Mr. Andersen," she greeted him, completely ignoring the man at her side because she was in crisis here—and it wasn't because old Bertha was playing up. "What are you doing up so early?"

"I'm always up early, missy. Fifty years of rising at dawn is a hard habit to break." He came forward and peered into the engine. "Know what you're doing there, sonny?"

"Yeah," Ty grunted, "but it's hard, doing it one-handed."

"Why don't you take the girl to work?" the old man suggested. "I'll see what I can do about *this* old girl."

"No!" Paige blurted out, freaking out a little at the thought of being stuck in the intimacy of a car with Mr. Bad Attitude for more than five seconds. "I'll just call Frankie. I'm sure she can—"

"That's a great idea, Mr. Andersen," Ty interrupted, sending Paige an inscrutable look as he brushed past her and gave her a rush to rival any she'd ever had for chocolate. "I'll just fetch my keys." And loped up the walk.

Paige shoved her fingers in her hair and considered doing an emergency chocolate run but she was too busy gaping after Tyler Reese…who'd disappeared through the door a few feet from hers.

What the heck was he doing, living right… next…door? How long had he been there and how had she not known? And another thing… why hadn't he told her?

But she knew. He'd wanted to be alone. Besides,

his father still owned the building and the adjacent unit *had* been empty for a couple of months. *He* probably also didn't want her getting any ideas about taking care of him. Or worse, that she would think they were a "thing".

As if.

He thought dating her was suicidal, for cripes' sake, and she...well, she *knew* it wasn't going to happen. *Ever.* Besides, the last thing she wanted was to crush on another unattainable guy like she had in the tenth grade. He might be sorry about what he'd said, but he was still a BAB. And BABs were trouble.

Big. Bad. Trouble.

"This old girl deserves better, missy." Harry interrupted her mental meltdown. "Worn pipes, frayed electrics...?" He tutted gruffly. "It's a wonder she hasn't blown up in your face."

Paige sighed. And right there was something else to add to her freak-out list because the news was about as welcome as discovering the sexiest guy in America thought she was an annoying pain in the ass.

Mentally crossing her fingers, she said as calmly as she could, "I know, I know. The question is, can she be saved?"

Please, please, please, say yes.

"Well... I can't say for sure," the old man admitted reluctantly, scratching his head. "The starter will have to be replaced and some other parts too if you really want to know."

Paige *really* didn't want to know but she gulped and asked bravely, "Will...will it be expensive, do you think, Mr. Andersen?" while frantically calculating the balance in her account and wondering if she was going to have to forgo eating for the next couple of weeks or dip into her meager savings.

For a moment Harry said nothing as he tightened a few more bolts. Then he straightened. "Now, don't you worry about a thing," he said, awkwardly giving her shoulder a rough pat just as Ty returned, car keys jingling. "I know Gus at the repair shop. I'll work out a good deal for you." Ty sauntered up, as if he had all the time in the world. "Off you go to work now, missy. You don't want to be late."

"I'll drive," Paige said, reaching out to snag Ty's keys. "You should be resting your shoulder. And don't worry about the car," she interrupted hurriedly when he looked like he might object. "I'll take good care of it and have it back by tonight."

His eyebrows rose up his forehead. "I'd be worried if it wasn't a rental," he drawled as she scurried off to grab her shoulder bag. "Considering the condition of yours."

Paige rolled her eyes and muttered through an interminable few minutes while she adjusted the seat. *Damn long-legged freaks.* And then when she finally turned the key, the SUV jerked forward a couple of yards and promptly stalled.

Snickering at the way Ty leapt out the way, the expression on his face priceless, Paige called out a strangled "Sorry" and managed to restart the car and shove it into gear without further embarrassing herself, giving Ty a coronary, or injuring more than just his pride.

She alternately snickered and moaned with embarrassment all the way to the medical center across town because if Tyler Reese had suspected her of being a crazy woman, he would now be certain.

Unfortunately, the morning shift was quiet, giving Paige way too much time to stew over the fact that he'd been living within feet of her the last few days and she hadn't known.

But then again maybe her subconscious had detected that potent combination of smoldering male pheromones and seething testosterone seeping through the wall because...well, because. Her breath whooshed out audibly, causing a nurse to send her a curious look.

Realizing it was the fifth time she'd sighed, Paige mentally slapped herself. *Okay, fine.* So she'd had a few hot dreams and a couple of bad moments in her shower imagining him—*yikes, her heart rate doubled and heat raced across her skin*—naked and running his hands all over her slick flesh.

She scowled at her body's traitorous response. *Big freaking deal.*

It didn't mean a thing because she'd had the same dreams about that black-haired guy who'd starred in a vampire TV series.

And then because she was fantasizing about lying on a warm deck while Ty and the vampire hottie massaged oil into her tingling skin, Paige tore out of Radiology, fanning herself with the report she was supposed to be reading.

And promptly collided with a large frame.

She gave a squeak of surprise and lurched backward, dropping the report. "Omigosh, Dr. Ch-Chapman, I'm s-so sorry," she spluttered in shock, blinking up into familiar blue eyes peering at her with concern. Familiar because just that morning she'd felt herself being drawn unwillingly into eyes that exact color.

She hoped, *really hoped* the medical director couldn't read minds.

"No need to apologize, Dr. Carlyle," the older man said cheerfully as he bent to retrieve her report, "Nothing serious, I hope."

Thinking he was referring to her hot thoughts about his...*gulp*...son, Paige fought the heat of embarrassment creeping into her cheeks. She bit lip and asked warily, "Why do you...um...ask?"

"It isn't every day I get bowled over by a beautiful young woman," he said, chuckling, nodding to the file he handed her.

Realizing he'd been talking about the report, Paige spluttered out a relieved laugh. "Oh, this. Um..." *Holy cow, she had to get a grip—especially in front of the big boss.* "A young patient fell off a trampoline onto his head," she explained breathlessly. "I was just on my way back from Radiology."

"Problem?"

"The X-ray detected an odd shadow. I don't think it's anything to worry about," she explained, "but I'm going to recommend a CT scan just to be safe."

"Excellent decision," he said, shrewd blue eyes twinkling at her. "I'm glad I ran into you." He chuckled a little at his own joke. "I heard you had a break-in the other night."

Paige gulped, fighting the heat of embarrassment creeping into her cheeks because the last thing she wanted to discuss with this man was the one she'd just been imagining naked.

Not that she had to imagine anything, especially as she'd already seen him naked. "Oh…um." She stifled a hysterical giggle and felt her face heat.

"Are you all right, Dr. Carlyle? You're looking a little flushed."

Her flush deepened. "It's… I…um, it's been a hectic day," she began, only to be interrupted by her pager. "Emergency," she explained after a quick look at the screen, hugely relieved to be saved by the pager.

He nodded. "Go see to that. We can talk another time," he said, and Paige bolted, wondering what the heck they had to talk about. That she'd given his son concussion and a dislocated shoulder? Or that she'd called the cops on him?

The ER shift supervisor grabbed Paige the instant she hurried through the doors. "There's been an accident up near Angel Lake Ranger station," he rapped out. "A school bus on the way back from a field trip left the road. Details are sketchy but it sounds like they slid off a sharp incline into a gully. Dispatch said there was a lot of screaming and it was difficult to get information."

Paige's heart clenched with dread. She hated it when little kids were hurt in accidents. "Is medevac on their way?"

"Climbing accident up in the mountains," Chalmers said impatiently. "You're up. They need someone to help with the kids."

"I've got a young patient who—" she said but he grabbed the report and gave her a nudge towards the ambulance bay doors.

"I'll take care of it. You. Go. Miss Bryce is waiting."

Paige took off. The bay doors whooshed open as she approached and she had a split second to register that an ambulance was idling in the bay, passenger door open and Frankie frantically beckoning.

Paige grabbed Frankie's hand and they took off, the momentum slamming the door closed behind her.

It wasn't unheard of for an ER doctor to accompany EMTs to the scene of an accident but it wasn't exactly standard operating procedure either.

Paige prayed they wouldn't find death today.

CHAPTER FIVE

STATE TROOPERS HAD already blocked off the road and were redirecting the sparse mid-afternoon traffic. They waved the ambulance on, and even before the vehicle screamed to a stop Frankie was leaping out.

Paige scrambled after her and headed for the edge of the road, where troopers were in discussion with forest rangers. Intent on getting to the trapped children, she didn't see the single figure not in uniform until she was almost upon him. At the sight of familiar wide shoulders, hard chiseled profile and dark wind-tousled hair she'd seen just that morning, her eyes widened and her step faltered.

What the heck was Tyler Reese doing here?

He must have sensed her scrutiny because he turned his head, his laser-bright gaze instantly locking onto her. If he was surprised to see her, it didn't show. Instead, he broke away from the group and headed towards her.

"You're here," he said briskly, taking her arm and pulling her aside.

"What are you doing here?" Paige asked absently, distracted by the skid marks swerving across the road and disappearing into the gap in the foliage. The bus was nowhere to be seen but from below she could hear the frantic cries of children and the soothing tones of male rescuers. Her heart squeezed.

"We came across the accident and stopped to help."

She made a move forward but Ty tugged her back.

"I need to get to those children, Tyler," she said, yanking on her arm. "They may be hurt."

He tightened his grip. "Nate's down there with a few rangers but we've got a bigger problem," he said in a tone that had Paige's head jerking up. He looked as grim as he sounded and her belly clenched in dread.

"What?"

"Most of the kids are fine. Some need medical attention but the paramedics can handle them."

"Then—"

"The teacher is trapped," he growled. "She was standing when the bus swerved across the road and rolled down into the gully. They managed to get to the children but she's pinned by crumpled metal."

"Can't they get her out?" Paige demanded, looking pointedly at the group milling around instead of acting. "Surely there's enough muscle here to move the obstacle?"

"They can't," he said bluntly, his eyes intent on hers. "Her arm is pinned. The minute they lift it she's going to bleed out."

Paige instantly understood Ty's implications. The metal was providing pressure and was keeping the teacher from bleeding out. The artery would have to be clamped before the weight was removed. There wasn't time to put pressure on the wound and transport her to a hospital. She would die before they got her up to the road.

"Well," she said briskly, "it's a good thing you're a surgeon, then, right?"

Ty's mouth twisted as he held up his casted hand. "Not happening, Dr. Carlyle. That's why I'm glad you're here. EMTs can't handle this procedure. It needs someone with surgical experience and knowledge."

Paige gaped at him then said in a fierce undertone, "Are you insane? I'm a pediatrician, not a surgeon. You, on the other hand, *are* one."

He held up his cast. "I can't use it," he reminded her tightly.

"Why didn't dispatch request a trauma surgeon? There's a very good reason I didn't choose surgery as my specialty."

One dark brow rose arrogantly. "You faint at the sight of blood?"

"Don't be ridiculous," she growled. "I work in ER." Ty's mouth curled very slightly at one corner.

"That's exactly what she's counting on. And they didn't request a trauma surgeon because at the time they didn't know they'd need one."

He let that sink in for a couple of beats, then taunted, "You going to let a fifth grade teacher bleed out, Doc? In front of her students?"

"Of course not," she snapped, furious with him for expecting her to perform something a trauma surgeon should do. Finally her breath escaped in an audible rush. "Fine," she said tightly. Maybe he couldn't actually perform the field surgery but he was going to guide her through it. "I'll do it but I need help."

Immediately his eyes shuttered and he turned away. "I'll get an EMT," he tossed over his shoulder.

But before he could take a couple of steps Paige snapped out, "Hold it right there, buster."

He froze and after a long moment turned his head, his expression a little stunned.

"Are you talking to me?"

Paige refused to back down. "You're the surgeon here, *Dr.* Reese," she reminded him shortly. "The EMTs are busy, remember. Taking care of the children."

His whole body recoiled as if she'd struck him. "No," he said coldly, and turned away.

"Yes," she insisted fiercely, hurrying after him. "You want me to do this then the least *you* can do is talk me through it."

At her words, he stopped abruptly and turned eyes as cold as the North Pacific on her. His entire body vibrated with tension. "I said no."

Paige caught the hollow misery behind the fury but couldn't let it deter her. "Dammit, *Dr.* Reese," she snapped. "You want a fifth grade teacher to die because you're mad at the world?"

"I am not mad—"

"You are. You're hurting and mad at everyone. Are you going to let that stop you from doing what you do best?"

"You don't know what I do best," he rasped, fury in the tight lines of his jaw and mouth. "Especially as I can't *do* a damned thing."

Holding his gaze with difficulty, she gave a casual shrug even as her heart pinched. Now wasn't the time to feel sorry for him. She needed him. The *teacher* needed him. "You've done it before, haven't you?" And when he just stared at her, she exhaled impatiently. "Well, then, we… I mean… you…" She chewed on her bottom lip and admitted in a fierce undertone, "*I've* never done it before."

His eyes blazing a promised retribution, Ty turned without another word and walked off.

"Hey!"

He paused and sent her a dark look over his shoulder. "Get going," he snarled. "I'll bring what you're going to need. And sometime, Dr. Carlyle, you're going to tell me what a pediatrician is doing working in ER."

Relief made her knees weak as she stumbled towards the troopers pulling fifth graders up by ropes. The whole exchange had taken less than a minute and it was another before she was wrapping her arms around a trooper and clinging to him like a monkey as they were lowered to the wreckage, wedged in by trees and rocks about fifty feet down.

Paige scrambled through the broken window and paused to cast an experienced eye over the children still left behind. She murmured encouragement as they clung to her, noting absently that Frankie had already set up triage and was studiously ignoring the man calmly and efficiently organizing the children.

Nate Oliver looked big and capable and just a little dangerous, as though he did this every day. But then again he did. He was a coastie.

"Dr. Cutie," he greeted her, looping the harness around a child before lifting him through the window. His voice, cheerful and upbeat for the children's benefit, dropped to a murmur meant for her ears only. "Glad you're here—she's barely hanging on."

Paige slid on the almost vertical floor and was grateful for his easy strength as he steadied her. He nodded to the front of the bus. "It's real bad," he reported softly. "T was about to turn me into a field surgeon but I don't think Grace Parker wants my version of first aid."

"You're a medic?"

"Nope, but I can get by in a pinch." He shook his head. "This is more like a giant squeeze. Have you seen him?"

"He's bringing med supplies."

Nate's eyes widened then sharpened, amusement and approval gleaming in the dark gaze. "He's coming down...here?"

"Not willingly," she admitted, and headed towards where a park ranger was crouched beside the teacher. Behind her she heard Nate laugh softly and say beneath his breath, "Well, well. This is going to be very interesting."

Yeah, well, she wouldn't exactly use the word "interesting". *Terrifying* would be closer to the mark, especially when she saw Grace Parker pinned to the side of the bus by a twisted mess of metal seats. Her white face was sweat-drenched and she had her teeth clenched against the pain.

"Hi," Paige said, moving as close as she could get, "I'm Paige."

"Yes," the woman rasped, her face tightening as she let slip a little moan. "I remember...you came to the school on health day."

Paige ran her eyes over Grace's pinned arm and estimated that she'd lost about five hundred ccs of blood—probably when rescuers had attempted to free her.

She squeezed the woman's free hand and noted that it was icy. They would have to hurry before she went into shock. "I've never had so many kids ask me about blood and guts before," she said, pressing her finger to the area above the injury site to feel for a pulse. "Or want to show me all their scars."

"They're a handful, all right." Grace breathed through another moan and grabbed Paige with her free hand. Her gaze was fever-bright with a dangerous edge of panic. "They're okay, aren't they? Please tell me they're okay."

"They're going to be fine, Grace. Scared mostly," she soothed. "But it's you we're all concerned about."

Her eyes closed briefly and she gave a short sobbing laugh. "I'm going to lose my arm, aren't I?"

A shadow blocked out the light and even before Ty eased into place beside her, she knew it was him. She had absolutely no idea why her senses were so attuned to him but her entire body went on alert.

Ignoring both it and him, she asked, "Why do you say that?"

"Keith—the ranger—said it was too dangerous to move me," Grace said tightly. Her eyes filled with tears. "B-but I... I have to tell you that I can't feel it. My arm, I mean. Tell them, Paige. Tell them to move this thing off me."

"We can't, Grace," Paige began, sparing a brief glance at Ty's hard, remote expression. He looked a little like he had the night of his attempted B&E, pale, clammy and his mouth set in a tight white line. His posture screamed anger and bad attitude. Whether at the situation or her, Paige couldn't tell. "The bar is stopping the bleeding."

"Try to relax," Ty said, crouching down near Grace's head and handing a bag to Paige. "And to make sure you don't move, even a fraction of an inch, Dr. Carlyle is going to give you a mild sedative."

Grace pressed her lips together and turned her face away. "I... I... It's bad, isn't it?"

Paige nibbled on her lip indecisively. Sometimes people wanted you to tell them everything was going to be okay and others needed to hear the bald truth.

Ty chose the truth.

"Yes, it's bad," he admitted calmly as Paige pulled on surgical gloves and reached for the sedative. "But it could be a lot worse," she heard him say. "I don't want you to worry now. Dr. Carlyle is a specialist and you couldn't be in safer hands."

Paige, swabbing an area on Grace's uninjured arm, glanced up briefly, thinking it was a good thing he'd failed to mention that she wasn't a trauma specialist or Grace would be as terrified as Paige. Instead of looking terrified, Grace's gaze was locked on Ty as though he was her lifeline and she was ready to do anything he asked.

Paige gave a mental eye-roll but then reluctantly admitted that she'd probably do anything he wanted if he spoke to *her* like that.

Which was kind of pathetic if you thought about it.

While she waited for the sedative to take effect, Paige wrapped a pressure cuff around Grace's arm and kept up a calm chatter when Ty took over.

Out the corner of her eye she saw his mouth tighten as he struggled one-handed but when she tried to help, he growled. She backed off, wondering if she'd done the right thing getting him down here, because it was clearly too much so soon after his accident.

But then his gaze—cool and clear—caught hers. He murmured, "You ready?"

And Paige felt her stomach drop and lift at the same time. *Oh, God, she really was going to do this.*

She exhaled slowly and nodded just as coolly. "Yes. You?" *Look at her, all calm and collected.*

Ty's eyebrow rose, as though he knew she was shaking in her sneakers. "I'm not the one about to perform a ligation in less than ideal conditions."

Great. So not the way to instill her with heaps of confidence.

"I can *do* this," she insisted with a lot more confidence than she felt. She wasn't a surgeon but she was the only person standing between her patient and death. She paused then said, "I'm ready."

His gaze searched hers for a long moment before he nodded. "Fine." His voice was brisk, professional. "The broken bar is gouging into the brachial artery midway up the humerus. Her pulse is weak so I want you to use a surgical glove as a tourniquet. Tie it a couple of inches above the injury site. It'll stop the bleeding long enough for you to clamp the artery."

Paige quickly obeyed.

With his left hand he sprayed the area with disinfectant. "Now, you're going to do an arterial cut-down at the point of impact. Using an eleven blade…no, that's a thirteen. The other one. Okay, now make an eight-centimeter longitudinal incision distal to the deep brachial confluence."

Paige positioned the scalpel and noticed her hands were shaking. She sucked in a sharp breath. *Dammit*, this was why she wasn't a surgeon. This was why—

A large warm hand engulfed hers.

"Paige." Ty's deep calm voice interrupted her mental panic. "Dr. Carlyle," he said again when she didn't respond, because she was in full freakout mode and trying to breathe without passing out.

"Look at me. Good," he said when she lifted her head. "Don't think about it. Just follow the sound of my voice and do exactly what I say. Okay?"

She dropped her gaze and tried to swallow past the growing panic in her throat.

"Hey." He leaned forward to catch her gaze. His eyes were no longer cold and remote but warmly encouraging, full of strength and confidence… in her. *Gulp*. "You'll be fine. Now say, 'I'm okay, Ty, I've got this.'"

She sucked in a shaky breath, licked dry lips and repeated, "I'm okay, Ty. I've got…" *gulp* "…this."

"Good." He gave her a hand a brief squeeze before letting go. "Without overthinking everything, let your training take over. Make the incision. Not too hard, just enough to cut through skin and muscle." Repeating his instructions in her head, Paige filtered out everything but the sound of his voice. "Excellent. Now push your fingers through the muscle until you feel the brachial artery…got it? Okay, gently palpate it to ensure it's not the cephalic vein or the median nerve. For God's sake, don't kink or sever that nerve or—"

"I'll cause paralysis. Yes, I know. Now what?"

His mouth twitched at her impatient tone. "Have you isolated the artery? Push aside the muscle with one hand and clamp the artery with the other." Clamps appeared in her field of vision and she fumbled a little as she took them. "Careful… you don't want it to rip. Have you got it?"

Paige rolled her eyes and looked around. "Yes, I've got it. Can we move her now?"

"No," he said, rising to his feet to beckon Nate and two rangers who'd stayed behind to help. "You can loosen the tourniquet and make sure that arm doesn't move. We haven't finished yet."

Paige twisted her body out of the way and immobilized Grace's arm while the men moved in. For an interminable moment the crumpled seats refused to budge until Ty muttered beneath his breath. Before Paige could open her mouth to tell him to stop, he gripped metal and pulled. There was a lot of grunting and swearing until the mangled metal finally gave way.

Grace Parker cried out as the pressure on her arm eased and Paige scrambled to cover her with her body. Eyes tightly closed, she waited for the entire mess to come snapping back...but after a couple of beats she heard Ty say, "*Dammit,* Paige, that was stupid."

Careful not to jostle the injured teacher, Paige spun around to tell him he was the idiot when she caught his involuntary grimace. Just then Grace gave a low moan and tried to sit up.

"Careful there," Paige soothed, gently applying pressure to keep her still. "Don't move. I'm not finished yet."

The teacher sucked in a sharp breath. "Did... did you have to c-cut it off?" she slurred, more than a little out of it.

"Nope," Paige said promptly. "It's still here." She quickly filled a syringe with pain meds while

Nate and Ty moved Grace to a more accessible area. "I'm giving you something for the pain and I want you to close your eyes and relax. We've got you."

Within seconds the woman had slipped away again and Paige readied herself to perform a ligation. She needed to do it quickly or the tissue would necrotize and Grace would lose her arm after all.

She irrigated the area and prepared the suture kit while Ty awkwardly swabbed the wound one-handed, then she clamped the other end and very carefully sutured the severed artery. When they got Grace back to the hospital the orthos would be waiting to repair the damage properly.

Once she was done, Ty slowly removed the first clamp, testing the integrity of the ligation. After a couple of beats Ty grunted his satisfaction and removed the second clamp so the blood flow could resume.

"Great job, Dr. Cutie," Nate said, giving her shoulder a tight squeeze. "You should have joined the army. You'd have made a kick-ass field surgeon."

Realizing she was still holding her breath, Paige let it go with an audible whoosh. She flashed a look at Ty to gauge his reaction but his face was set in a hard unreadable mask.

Yeah. So much for, "Great job, Paige, I couldn't have done better." Realizing she'd been waiting for his approval, Paige shook her head at herself and inflated the BP cuff. Everyone held their breaths as the needle fell...and fell...finally bobbing at around seventy.

"Better," Ty murmured, and rose, turning away to hide his involuntary wince. But for some reason she was becoming an expert on Ty Reese body language. He'd clearly wrenched his shoulder again.

Men!

Planning to catch him before she went back to the hospital, Paige quickly finished up, but by the time Frankie and Dale moved in to take over, he'd vanished.

Slouched low in his chair, Ty propped his feet on the deck railing, wincing as pain lanced through his shoulder. He needed to get ready for dinner with his father but moving meant using muscles he'd abused earlier today.

Lifting the beer bottle to his mouth, he admitted a little ruefully that maybe he'd been an idiot to help move those seats. But he'd seen Paige do what needed to be done without turning a hair. What else could he do but be a man?

He hated to admit it, but she'd been right about him. He *was* mad at the world. Mad that he'd been forced to rely on the skills of someone else to save his hand. Mad that he was living in a limbo caused by a drunken idiot who'd ploughed into a crowd of theatergoers because Ty looked like someone he had a grudge against. Mad that everything continued as though his world hadn't come crashing down.

But at least he was walking, he thought with self-disgust. One victim of the hit-and-run had died and at least another had a crushed pelvis. He had no right to feel as though he was the only one affected by one man's drunken rage.

Yet Paige hadn't hesitated to put herself between her patient and danger. She'd wanted nothing more than to be there for her young patients but she'd stepped in because…because he was a coward and there'd been no one else.

Then Nate had complimented her and suddenly Ty couldn't get away fast enough. He'd been filled with such self-loathing that he'd snarled at Nate's suggestion that he have his shoulder checked out.

He didn't need anyone to tell him he'd torn something. He was still a doctor, damn it. And no one was going to bully him into anything he didn't want and wasn't ready for—especially a feisty little medic with big eyes, a soft mouth and an even softer heart.

The memory of her stiff spine and huge hazel eyes filled with challenge and reproof as she'd squared off with him made him smile. She might look like a strong wind would blow her away but she was tougher and…he chuckled…meaner than she looked.

A whisper of sound caught his attention a beat before light spilled onto the deck and the person he'd been thinking about opened the French doors and stepped outside.

She looked towards his darkened sitting room and must have noticed that his French door was open because she stomped towards it, muttering about people leaving an "open invitation to the crazies of this world".

"Need something?"

She uttered an ear-piercing shriek and stumbled back a couple of steps, nearly falling over a deck-chair. "*Dammit*," she swore, catching herself.

"Stop *doing* that!" For a few moments her heavy breathing filled the darkness, reminding him of things he hadn't had in a while. Things he'd convinced himself this morning that he didn't feel for Paige Carlyle.

Things that should have scared him into escaping back to California but which kept him glued to the lounger because he was tired of running. She stomped closer and demanded, "What the heck are you doing, sitting out here? It's freezing."

He reached out, snagged her hand and pulled.

She gave a startled "Oomph," and tumbled right into his lap. "What—what are you *doing*?" she squeaked, as light from her apartment spilled over her shocked face.

And then Ty did what he'd told himself he didn't want. He swooped down and crushed her soft mouth with his. He'd meant it as punishment for everything she'd put him through but the instant his mouth touched hers he wanted more.

A lot more.

To prevent her from escaping, he slid his left hand up her back and buried his fingers in her cool, soft hair. She uttered a muffled protest and made to push away but Ty tightened his grip, opening his mouth over hers to snatch her breath, silence her protest.

His sudden intensity must have startled her because she gasped, and he took advantage by thrusting his tongue into her warm, wet mouth.

He tasted surprise and something hot and hungry and suddenly he was desperate for the taste of her in his mouth and the feel of her naked skin against his. And then even if he'd wanted to, he couldn't have stopped because she suddenly straddled him and he was seeing more stars than there were currently in the night sky. The move surprised him and he was abruptly harder than he'd ever been in his life—in less than two seconds flat.

She took advantage of his momentary surprise by fisting both hands in his hair and dragging him closer, as though she was afraid he'd try to escape. But Ty wasn't going anywhere. Instead, he slid both arms around her and responded with a hunger that might have shocked him if he'd been able to do more than growl with the need clawing at his gut.

Things went a little crazy then as Ty kissed her the way he liked it, hot and wet and deep. She made little mewling sounds and responded, closing her teeth around his tongue.

It made him grin and slide his hand up her back to cup her head. When he finally ran out of air, he broke away to graze his lips across her jaw towards the soft skin just below her ear.

She tasted like temptation, soft and delicious... so delicious that he found himself humming in the back of his throat and testing another patch of skin.

She was breathing like she'd just swum across the strait, and since he was too, he punished her by biting down on the tender lobe he'd exposed.

She jolted, her fingers clenching reflexively. Since they were still buried in his hair, the sharp pain made him nip her again until a delicate shudder moved through her. She made little huffing sounds that shouldn't have turned him on but did—and began rolling her hips, the hottest, softest part of her pressing into the hardest part of him.

In no time he was shuddering and huffing because... *Holy cow*, she was the sexiest thing he'd ever kissed and he was suddenly desperate to feel all her softness beneath him, feel her around him as he thrust home.

With one thought—to get them both naked—
Ty made to roll her beneath him. The move had
him sucking in air as sharp pain tore through his
shoulder. He stilled, hoping it would go away because there was no way he was stopping now.

But Paige must have heard that involuntary
sound of pain because she froze. "What—?" she
gasped, looking as stunned as he felt. "What's
wrong?"

"Nothing."

His gaze dropped to her swollen mouth and he
tried to pull her back but fire engulfed his shoulder and he couldn't suppress a groan.

"I knew it," she said breathlessly, scrambling
off his lap and making his eyes cross because...
Holy cow. "You're hurting."

He huffed out a laughing curse and grabbed her
hand to keep her from escaping, drawing her between his knees. He grimaced and shifted to ad-
just his position. "Then why are we stopping?"

She must have seen the direction of his gaze
because she uttered a startled snort. "Not that,
dummy," she wheezed huffily, and yanked her
arm free. "Your shoulder. You hurt it again."

"What? No, it's just a little stiff, that's all."

Paige pressed her lips together but a weird

grunting kind of snort escaped. She tried to look innocent but Ty had no trouble following her train of thought because his erection was still pressed against her.

"Okay," he admitted with an unabashed grin. "So 'little' is a gross misrepresentation but I was actually referring to my shoulder, Miz I'm-not-so-sweet-and-innocent."

She rolled her eyes, not looking the least bit offended by the name. "I grew up with three older brothers," she said, pointing an accusing finger at him. "And stop trying to distract me. I was also talking about your shoulder. Not…" She waved her hand at his lap. "Not that."

Chuckling, he tried to roll his shoulder and had to suck in a sharp breath. Okay, so maybe it was a little more than stiff. Not that he would admit it, though.

"You're lying. You tried to be a macho hero today and tore something, didn't you?"

Irritated and hurting in more than one area of his anatomy, Ty rolled off the lounger and rose. "Quit nagging, I'm fine. Now," he growled, moving stiffly towards the open French door, "if you'll excuse me, I'm going out."

"To the hospital, I hope," she huffed, following as he headed inside.

He scoffed, "Don't be ridiculous," and turned to block her path with a big arm across the doorway. "I'm a trauma surgeon. I know how to treat an injury."

She canted her hip and folded her arms beneath her breasts. "Fine, then you won't mind if I see it."

For a moment he was irritated as all hell; then he slowly allowed his mouth to curl, instinctively knowing how to distract her. "Why didn't you just say so?" he drawled, enjoying the play of emotions across her face.

Paige stared at him for a couple of beats, her brow wrinkled in confusion, but Ty knew the instant she caught on because her mouth dropped open and a wild flush bloomed beneath her skin.

"You…you…*guy*," she stuttered, looking as though she didn't know whether to laugh or hit him. Finally, she huffed out an exasperated breath and spun away. "Fine," she snapped, stomping off, muttering, "I hope it falls off."

Before she could slam the door, Ty called out, "My arm or…?"

In a thrice it whipped open and she yelled, "Use your imagination." She was about to disappear but stuck her head out to snap, "And another thing. Wear a damn bell or quit sneaking up on me. Next time I might be holding a carving knife."

Ty was chuckling when her door finally slammed. He waited a couple of seconds, half expecting another insult, but her light was switched off, leaving the deck in darkness.

Leaving Ty alone.

Yeah, he thought as his amusement faded. Exactly how he wanted it.

Wasn't it?

CHAPTER SIX

A WEEK LATER, Paige arrived home and made a beeline for the kitchen. It had been a crazy day and she'd barely had time to think, let alone eat or catch a minute for a break.

She put on coffee and opened the overhead cabinet before remembering that she'd used the last mug that morning.

Muttering about her lax housekeeping skills, she kicked off her shoes and headed for the deck. She vaguely remembered seeing the rest of the mugs scattered there, mostly because she tended to get sidetracked in the morning and kept leaving them either on the deck railing, the steps, or on the wooden patio table.

But when she opened the French doors she found all eight mugs on the table, sparkling clean as though waiting for her to bring out the coffee.

Her eyes widened. And that wasn't all. The beach towels she'd draped over the wooden deck chairs to air out a few days ago were neatly folded beside the mugs.

Eyebrows rising up her forehead, Paige looked around to thank the cleaning fairies and found a half-naked Ty sprawled in the lounger, fast asleep.

Without her permission, her gaze swept over that wide, tanned expanse of awesomely sculpted chest to the eight-pack abs she'd been dreaming about licking...*phew*...and the happy trail that disappeared into a pair of faded low-slung jeans.

To her absolute horror her nipples tightened and her knees wobbled. She grabbed the back of the nearest chair to keep from falling and told herself it was hypoglycemia giving her such a head rush.

He, on the other hand, looked disgustingly healthy—not to mention *really* hot—and relaxed, and the fading bruises were barely visible on his sun-warmed skin. She glared at him and barely resisted the urge to grab the pitcher of water beside him and cool him the heck off.

"Don't even think about it," he warned in a voice rough and deep with sleep.

Pulse bumping up a couple notches, Paige screwed up her face. It was the first time she'd seen him since the night of "The Kiss" and despite trying very hard not to, she'd found herself worrying—and thinking—about him at the most inconvenient times. Worrying about his shoulder, his hand and…and darn it, she worried that he wasn't taking care of himself.

Which was really stupid and girly. Of course he could take care of himself. He was all grown up. She gulped and mentally fanned herself. Especially in nothing but those low-slung faded jeans that drew her eyes like a magnet because they lovingly cupped him in cuppable places.

"Think about what?" she asked in an attempt at innocence, but either Tyler Reese could read minds or she wasn't a very good actress. One arched brow made her suspect the latter.

His mouth curved as he swept his sleepy blue gaze over her. She'd had some pretty hot dreams about that mouth, *dammit,* as well as his broad shoulders…wide chest…washboard abs…lower— Dreams she'd awakened from all sweaty, flustered and extremely frustrated.

"What?" she demanded, conscious of the fact that while he looked rested and relaxed, she was feeling—and probably looking like—the effects of a hectic week.

He yawned and scrubbed a hand down his face.

"You try throwing water on me and you won't like my reaction."

"I'm not worried," she said smugly. "Look at you, getting soft with all the lazing around. I took you down once and I can do it a—" Her words ended on a shocked squeak when she found herself beneath him on the lounger. He'd moved so fast she hadn't seen it coming until she was flat on her back with his big, hard body covering hers.

She blinked and found his lean dark face a couple inches above hers. "Wha...?" A delicious heat and lethargy invaded her limbs.

No, darn it. Not delicious, a voice yelled in her head. *Dangerous. And unwelcome.*

Yeah, Paige, unwelcome...because...because... *Oh, boy.* She sucked in a lungful of warm delicious man and couldn't for the life of her recall... What was she supposed to remember again?

"You were saying?" Ty smirked as though he could read her thoughts and all she could do was swallow and say, "Huh?"

At her eloquent response, Ty gave a crooked grin that was far too appealing for her liking.

"Look at you." He snickered, mimicking her. "All flustered and flushed, and my personal favorite...speechless."

"If I'm……speech-less, you big lug," she pretend-wheezed, "it's…because… I…can't…breathe."

He immediately shifted his weight to his un-injured elbow but instead of allowing Paige to breathe easier, it pressed a certain part of his anat-omy—a very long, thick, hard part—into a cer-tain corresponding part of her anatomy.

And look at that—she lost her breath, this time for real.

"You're…um…" She broke off and squirmed, her face heating when he just grinned.

"Just ignore it."

"Oh, right." Paige spluttered out a laugh. Like that was even possible with that…yes, *that* jab-bing her in the thigh. Or the hard, flat *naked* belly against hers. Or the way his thigh pressed against her— *How the heck had he sneaked a leg be-tween hers?*

"Seriously," he advised as though she wasn't al-ready melting. "Don't give it another thought… unless…"

She stilled, her eyes narrowing suspiciously. "Unless what?"

"Unless you wanna check it out," he said casu-ally, his eyes beginning to crinkle at the corners.

"What? No," she gasped in outrage, giving his

shoulders a bad-tempered shove, moving him…
nowhere. "Is that how you charm your women,
Reese? Play doctor and get them to give you
a…a…physical?"

"I was talking about my shoulder," he said
dryly, and with one economic move rolled off the
lounger and rose to his feet. Huffing like a steam
engine—because no way had he meant that—
Paige found herself admiring the play of muscles
beneath all that smooth warm skin. Flesh that
until a second ago had been so close she'd have
been able to lean forward and lick it.

"You planning on sleeping, Dr. Cutie?" Ty asked
over one wide shoulder.

"Call me that and die," she said sleepily, prop-
ping her head on her hand and transferring her
gaze to the view the deck afforded of the sea, harbor and marina. "But to answer your last question, I think I might. Not all of us get to nap in
the afternoon. But… I see why you like it here.
It's beautiful."

"It sure beats watching what passes for daytime
television around here," he said dryly, scratching his naked chest and stretching the kinks out
of his back. Finding her attention locked on his

chest—again—she shifted her gaze and caught sight of the mugs.

That reminded her of food.

"You didn't happen to see any faeries cleaning the deck while you were lazing the day away, did you?" she asked, rolling to her feet with a big yawn. "I'd like to thank them."

"You're welcome."

Surprised and a little confused, she blinked up at him. "Huh?"

"I said you're welcome."

It took Paige a couple seconds to compute. "You?" she said, gaping at him. "You're the—?"

"Cleaning faerie."

Immediately an image of Tyler Reese dressed in a pink tutu, tights, wings and a crown popped front and center in her mind. Before she could stop it, a snort emerged and by the expression on his face—speechless and a little pissy—her reaction was clearly as unwelcome as it was unexpected.

She slapped a hand over her mouth to stifle her amusement but it just grew and grew until it finally burst out of her. In seconds she was howling with laughter.

In fact, she laughed so much she had to sit down,

plopping back down on the lounger. After a few minutes she calmed down enough to see through tears of mirth. His expression of annoyed exasperation mixed with reluctant amusement nearly set her off again but she managed to keep it to a couple of strangled chuckles. Finally she sighed and wiped her eyes. She hadn't laughed like that in ages. It felt good. Almost as good as seeing him at a loss for words. She bet that didn't happen very often.

"You about done?" he inquired politely.

She grinned up at him, all her previous fatigue forgotten.

"I bet you look awesome in a pink tutu and tights." She ran her eyes over his wide, sculpted chest and shoulders and had to remind herself that Tyler Reese was the hottest thing she'd seen since she'd been seventeen and her brother Quinn had brought home a SEAL friend for the holidays. She'd stupidly fallen for a pretty face and a hot body, only to have her heart broken when he'd pursued everything with breasts. Everything except her, of course.

She cringed at the memory of practically throwing herself at him, although to be fair she'd been a little young—and a lot inexperienced—for him. But he'd barely noticed when she'd worn her brand-new bikini, ruffling her hair like she'd been six or something. She'd made sure it was the last time she'd been home when one of her brothers brought home a friend.

Fortunately she wasn't seventeen and had had a few—some kind of serious—relationships over the years but she wasn't stupid enough to fall for another BAB because of sexy blue eyes and a warm hard body.

No way...no matter how good a kisser he was.

Good? Try out-of-this-world spectacular. But guys like Ty Reese and Dean Walker barely noticed her beyond the fact that she was Quinn's cute little sister...or...or the annoying neighbor they wanted to ignore.

She sighed. *Yep. Story of her life.*

Because she couldn't take all eight mugs at once, Paige hurried into the house with four and made a beeline for the kitchen. The coffee was finished and a delicious aroma filled the air, reminding her that she'd barely eaten all day. Her stomach growled loudly.

"Caffeine, then I promise to feed you," she muttered to her stomach. Or maybe a cold shower, she thought, rolling her eyes at the blood still pump-

ing through her veins at warp speed. The darned
man was potent and the only way to keep her
heart safe was to avoid him like mildew.

She poured coffee into her favorite mug, turning
to the fridge for milk, and promptly collided with
a human wall. She lurched back with a shriek and
bumped into the counter, spilling scalding coffee
over her hand.

She managed a painful gasp before Ty whisked
the mug away and shoved her whole hand and half
her arm under the cold tap.

"What—what the heck are you doing?" She
gaped up at him as water splashed everywhere.

"That was careless of you," he murmured deeply
into her hair, sending an army of goose-bumps
marching down her spine. And because it left her
backed into the corner of the counter, surrounded
by delicious masculine heat, the goose-bumps
morphed into arrows of heat pinging in her belly.

Oh, heck, no.

"Me?" she demanded on an outraged squeak as
she tried to yank her hand free. *No tingling, pinging or melting allowed, dammit.* "What did I tell
you about sneaking up on me?"

He sent her a chiding look that said she should

be thanking him, not giving him a hard time. *Yeah, right.*

"Fortunately you're not holding a knife."

"I could always get one," she muttered defensively. "Fortunately for you I'm too hungry to fight with you."

He gave a soft grunt and muttered something that sounded like, "Too bad, I wouldn't mind seeing you try." And reached over to snag a kitchen towel. With her palm gently cradled in his he proceeded to dry her hand and arm. "It's a little red but no permanent damage done. You should be more careful."

"I wouldn't have to be careful if people stopped sneaking up on me," she muttered, her gaze on the dark silky head bent over her hand. Her fingers looked pale and delicate in his, making her feel excruciatingly feminine and, darn it, sending sensation zipping up her arm.

He looked up then and before she knew it, she was drowning in his startling blue eyes.

"Um…" she said, locking her knees against the urge to melt at his feet—wouldn't he just love that? His pupils widened until only a thin ring of blazing blue remained and before she knew it her mind went utterly blank.

Finally he took a step back and shoved a hand through his hair, rumpling the already tousled strands. "Why don't...?" He cleared his throat and tried again. "Why don't you change out of those... um, wet scrubs and I'll take you to dinner?"

Paige's eyes widened at the unexpected invitation. "You mean like a...a *date*?" But when his answer was to turn and stare at her as though she'd suggested something illegal, Paige cringed inside, wishing she could recall her words. *Yeesh.* Was she a sucker for punishment or what?

"No, I mean like dinner...between..." His breath whooshed out and he looked a little panicked. "I mean, you're hungry, I'm hungry and I'd like... I've seen the contents of your refrigerator." And when she continued to stare at him, he growled, "Dammit, you want dinner or not?"

"I want," she said primly, secretly pleased that she'd managed to rattle him because—if she wasn't mistaken—he'd definitely been about to kiss the socks off her. "But I warn you, I'm starving. And I want dessert."

A dark brow rose up his forehead. "Dessert?"

"Yep." She nodded, pushing away from the counter and heading for the door. "And wine. Lots of wine."

* * *

Ty took her to a steak house on the waterfront, mostly because he was craving steak and the Surf 'n Turf served the best in town, but also because it had a great view of the harbor.

Okay, and maybe he'd been a little bored and was looking for company. He, Tyler Reese, king of the I-want-to-be-aloners was sick to death of his own company. He needed a distraction and who better to distract him than his very distracting neighbor?

She was sexy and feisty and she made him smile when he hadn't felt like smiling for a long time. There was just something about her that drew him in despite himself. Earlier on the deck he'd wanted to kiss her more than he'd wanted his next breath and the overwhelming impulse to take her there in front of the entire marina had scared him.

Okay, try terrified, because Paige Carlyle didn't strike him as the fling type. His parents should never have married, partly because his father was a workaholic and forgot he had a family but mostly because his mother didn't know the meaning of compromise. She'd grown up wealthy and had expected Henry Chapman to keep her in the style to which she'd been accustomed. And while he'd tried, by working around the clock, she'd resented any time he spent away from her.

For a long time Ty had resented that too because he'd had to live with the fallout when his mother's marriages imploded. As a kid he'd been dragged from one house and stepfather to the next. He'd had no say in any of it and had vowed that once he grew up *he'd* be the one in control.

His accident had made him feel like a kid again, helpless against the whims of others. So he'd take Paige to dinner and when he left her at her door at the end of the evening, that would be that.

He'd stay away—for good this time.

It was still early and the dinner crowd was thin but Paige looked around with interest, giving Ty the impression that she hadn't been there before. Why that idea appealed to him, he had no idea. It wasn't even like this was a real date.

A bouncy teenager dressed in jeans and a Surf 'n Turf golf shirt approached and cheerfully asked where they would like to sit. She took one look at Ty and blushed, fumbled the menus and blushed even more when she dropped them.

Paige bent to help and with a quick laugh rose to her feet, chattering about how she'd love a view of the harbor. The waitress hurried over to a window table and stuttered when she handed Ty a menu and nearly took out his eye.

After she left, Paige said reproachfully, "You scared her."

"Me? What did I do?"

"You're wearing your inscrutable surgeon's face. Some people find it scary."

Clearly she didn't consider herself "some people" because she never hesitated to tell him off. He found it a refreshing change from all the people—women especially—who wanted to appease him.

Paige Carlyle didn't strike him as an appeaser.

"You mentioned something the other day about growing up with three brothers."

"Uh-huh."

After a couple of beats of silence, he reached out a finger and pushed the plastic-coated menu down until he could see her eyes. He raised an eyebrow, surprised by her shuttered expression when she was usually so easy to read.

"What?"

"Mother, father, brothers?"

She tried to tug her menu away but when he held on, she growled at him.

"Fine," she said huffily. "Dad is living with his new wife and family in Tacoma. Bryn is the manager of a San Diego football team, Eric's a Navy SEAL and Quinn's in the Air Force."

"And your mother? Is she also remarried?"

"No," she said flatly, a faint frown marring the smooth skin of her forehead. "She...um...she died when I was young."

"I'm sorry," he said quietly, dropping his hand. "I can see that it's still painful."

"Yes, well." She gave a ragged laugh. "What was even more painful was that less than two years later my father remarried and I suddenly had another family I didn't need or want." She shook her head. "He didn't even wait two years before...well, never mind," she dismissed quickly, taking a gulp of water the waitress had delivered. "I'm sure you don't want to hear the boring details of my sad and lonely adolescence."

She drew in a shaky breath and he could see her shake off her painful thoughts. When she next looked at him her eyes were huge and liquid in the soft lighting as they met his and he felt himself fall just a little bit. Before he could catch himself, she asked, "What about you?"

Huh? "Me?"

"How bad is it?"

He shook his head to dispel the notion that

she was bewitching him and that he was letting her. He stilled, a thread of panic winding its way through his chest. *Not just no way, but no way in hell*. He was letting the atmosphere—and memories of his own sad and lonely childhood—affect him, that's all.

"It?"

She lowered her lashes and the lacy pattern they made on her cheeks drew his fascinated gaze until she murmured, "Your injury," abruptly jolting him out of the sensual haze she was spinning with her eyes.

Cursing himself for behaving like a love-struck adolescent, Ty hitched a shoulder. "Only time will tell," he said casually to hide the churning in his gut. *Dammit*. He needed to get a grip before Little Miss Medic had him rolling over and begging for treats.

Tyler Reese, rising trauma surgeon, didn't beg for anything from anyone…least of all women. He was in control. Like always.

She nibbled on her lip, clearly wanting to say something more. And just when he thought she was going to offer her sympathy—or, worse, get him to talk about his feelings—she said, "So, you really washed my mugs and cleaned the deck?"

He sighed, a mix of relief, gratitude and impatience that she was still an annoying pain in the ass. "Why should that surprise you?"

She shrugged, flashing him a guilty look before retreating behind her menu. "No reason," she said quickly. "No reason at all except…"

"Except what?"

"Well, you're a surgeon," she said impatiently, as though that was reason enough.

Tired of talking to plastic, he whipped the menu away and demanded, "What does being a surgeon have to do with cleaning up after myself?"

"Well, technically it was cleaning up after me," she said primly, and when he just stared at her, Paige continued. "You have to ask? Really?" She sighed. "Fine. Surgeons don't exactly have a reputation for cleaning up messes. They swoop in like demi-gods, save the injured and dying with their mad, awesome skills and then disappear, leaving the grunt work to the rest of us peons."

"*Us* peons? You're a pediatrician. What's peonish about that?"

She sniffed and stole his menu out from under his nose. "Surgical rotation," she explained, looking pleased with her sneakiness. She was silent a couple of beats before saying casually, "So did you?"

Confused by her rapid changes of direction, he asked, "Did I what?"

She rolled her eyes like he was being deliberately obtuse. "Wash my mugs and clean my deck."

"Technically the deck is half-mine—okay, fine," he sighed, scrubbing a hand down his face. "The place was a mess. All I did was stick the mugs in the dishwasher and pay a kid ten bucks to clean the deck. No big deal."

She choked and stared at him, her eyes going huge. "T-ten bucks? You paid a kid *ten bucks* to clean the deck? *Yeesh. I* would have done it for ten bucks."

He snorted but before he could point out that she was a specialist and must be earning good money, the waitress arrived to take their order.

He ordered wine and the biggest rare steak on the menu with a side salad while Paige ordered the lady's steak with fries and vegetables. When the food came, Ty watched her face light up as she tucked right in. Clearly she hadn't been kidding about being starved.

After a few seconds she realized he was staring at her and paused with her fork halfway to her mouth.

"What?" she demanded, looking like she'd been

caught with her hand in the cookie jar. "I'm hungry, okay?" She grimaced and put down her fork as though realizing she'd been almost inhaling her food. "ER was so busy today I didn't get a chance to eat or drink," she said a little defensively.

"What are you doing in ER if you've already specialized in pediatrics?"

Paige's sigh did amazing things to the simple cut of her bodice and just about fried a couple of billion brain cells. Brain cells that he would need if he was going to have to make tough decisions about his future...or resist the sensual web she was spinning around him.

Completely oblivious to his burgeoning brain aneurysm, she said, "Money," on a rush of expelled air and a flush of embarrassment.

"Money?" He was surprised. He hadn't pegged her as the kind of woman who'd pursue a career for money. But, then, he'd been wrong about women before, so what the hell did he know? "Surely you can't be earning much here. In fact, I know that working in the city would pay a hell of a lot more."

An odd look clouded her features before she reluctantly admitted, "It's not that." She was silent a moment before shrugging and picking up her fork to poke at her food. "I had a scholarship so..."

"Ah." He nodded in comprehension. "So you have to go where they tell you."

"Yes. Fortunately, I was sent here." She turned to look at the scene outside the restaurant window. Lights lit up the harbor and boardwalk, reflecting off the water and the boats moored there. He knew without looking what she saw. A pretty, picturesque town nestled between the Straits of Juan de Fuca and the Olympic National Park. "I know someone who was sent to a one-horse town in the middle of nowhere where mountain men grunt, spit and scratch themselves in public. Believe me, this is paradise."

She pushed her plate aside and before he knew what she was doing she'd pulled his plate closer and was cutting his steak into bite-size pieces. "I have another year to go and until then I have to put in my time in ER where I'm needed."

A little disconcerted by her actions, he said absently, "I can speak to my father—"

"No," she said firmly, interrupting him before he could finish his sentence. "Thank you, but a contract is a contract. Besides, I've got this."

Amusement and admiration warred with exasperation at her fierce independence. "I'm sure you have," he said mildly. "But it's not a sign of weakness to accept help once in a while."

"It is if it comes with strings," she retorted.

"Strings?" He was confused for a couple of beats and then his jaw dropped at her implication. "You think my father would...?" The idea was shocking and something he'd never, *never* considered. Could Henry Chapman be capable...?

"What? *No!*" She gaped at him, clearly just as shocked by his suggestion. "What a terrible thing to say about your own father."

He was mollified by her angry denial until he thought of something else that made his stomach cramp. "You can't mean that *I* would...?"

"No!" A wild flush of horror and mortification heated her cheeks. "I didn't mean *that* either," she muttered, attacking the steak with renewed vigor. *"Jeez."*

Thoroughly confused, Ty searched Paige's expression for clues about what she meant but she'd hidden behind a swing of silky black hair. "Then what the hell *did* you mean?" he demanded.

Without replying, she shoved his plate back across the table, glaring at him as though he'd suggested something indecent. Which, of course, he had and it had completely freaked him out thinking of his father and— No, not going to think about…that.

Too freaky.

Another thing that was *just* as disturbing was thinking about Paige with someone who'd demand payment for doing a small favor.

It made him wonder what kind of men she knew.

"Only as a general statement, *yeesh*. All I'm saying is that generally if people do someone a favor they expect something in return. Besides…" she waved her fork in the air "…guys don't…" She stopped abruptly. Face flaming, she dropped her gaze to stab bad-temperedly at her steak.

Ty leaned back in the booth, fascinated by the myriad emotions chasing across her delicate features. "Well, don't stop there, Dr. Cutie," he drawled. "Not when this conversation is getting so very interesting." He waited for her reaction and when it came—in the form of a poisonous glare—he prompted, "Guys don't what?"

Her soft mouth firmed. "Nothing."

Leaning across the table, he repeated, "Guys don't what?"

"Think of me that way, okay?" she snapped,

pressing her lips together as though to prevent any more secrets from spilling out. "Happy now?"

Baffled, he studied her mutinous expression, searching for clues to her thoughts, and when she stubbornly remained silent, he asked mildly, "And what way is that?"

Her reply was a huge eye–roll, as though he was the dumbest person alive. Hiding a smile, he picked up his fork and speared a succulent piece of steak. "I hate to disagree with you," he said dryly, "but guys most *definitely* think of you that way."

CHAPTER SEVEN

BY THE TIME they left the restaurant, Paige was feeling pleasantly mellow. Whether it was from the excellent wine or the heat of Ty's body as he steered her towards his SUV, she couldn't tell, only that she felt relaxed for the first time in months. Years, maybe.

Okay, maybe not relaxed, she amended, catching sight of his hard profile and sculpted mouth in the dash glow. Buzzed. Like there was some weird energy source humming just beneath her skin.

It might have alarmed her if she'd been thinking clearly but she was still surprised by how much she'd enjoyed their spirited conversation—everything from her favorite toothpaste to the correct procedure for handling difficult patients.

She must have dozed off because the next thing she knew someone was shaking her. Muttering irritably, she tried to turn over but something had her pinned.

She frowned and opened her eyes, blinking in

the light shining through the windshield. In the next instant she recognized... "Ty?"

She sat up and looked around, noting that they were parked in the street in front of the house. Her neighbor, looking big and badass, stood beside her open door, his face in darkness.

Her heart gave a funny little flutter that she told herself was alarm but she couldn't quite convince herself.

"Whaddid I miss?" she slurred, shoving a hand through her hair in an attempt to wake up.

"Here I thought my scintillating conversation had left you speechless," he drawled, and reached for her seat belt, "when all the while you were snoring."

She stuck her tongue out at him. "If it makes you feel better," she said, sliding out only to stumble against him, "I don't fall asleep on just anyone, you know."

She was almost certain it wasn't deliberate, but when he steadied her by pulling her against him, she decided to stay there a few moments longer to test her theory. Dropping her forehead against his warm solid chest, she gave a hum of pleasure because she couldn't remember the last time anyone had held her. Or the last time she'd *let* anyone hold her, never mind lean on them.

It was kind of nice.

She shivered. *Fine, so maybe nice wasn't quite the right—*

"You falling asleep there, Dr. Cutie?"

Okay, Paige thought with an inner sigh. *Moment over.*

She gave him a half-hearted punch for his transgression and shoved away. "I hate that name," she muttered, turning to stomp down the path and up the porch stairs. "I *really* hate that name. And the next person to call me that is gonna be sorry."

She stopped in front of her door and reached into her purse for her keys, sparing him an annoyed glance when he joined her. He was mostly in darkness but light from the single wall-sconce illuminated half his face, highlighting one cheekbone, his strong jaw and the deep bow of his top lip.

His mouth was smiling, suggesting he enjoyed baiting her.

She yanked out the front door key and pointed it at him accusingly. "You're lucky you have such a pretty mouth," she announced. "Or I might be tempted to punch it."

He chuckled softly. "Men don't have pretty mouths," he said, snagging the key and inserting it in the lock. The door swung open and when she didn't move, he propped his shoulder against the frame, his gaze amused, patient.

"*You* do," she insisted, stepping close. Reaching out a finger, she traced the sculpted lines she suddenly wanted on hers more than she'd wanted anything, including that last mouthful of decadent chocolate dessert.

It took a moment to realize he'd stilled and when she did she abruptly dropped her hand and spun away, eager to pretend the rejection hadn't stung. Ty caught her hand and used it to tug her around. "That wasn't a rejection," he murmured, lifting her hand to his mouth.

At the move her eyes flew up and he held her gaze as he gently bit down on the soft pad of her finger.

Tingles instantly shot up her arm, and her knees wobbled. "What…?"

"That," he murmured, taking a nip out of another finger, "was surprise you didn't slug me. And just so we're clear here, there is *nothing* pretty about me."

His voice, deep and velvet-soft rasped against

her flesh and spread delicious warmth across her flesh. "*You,* on the other hand…" his arm snaked around her and he yanked her against him hard enough to knock a startled gasp from her "…are pretty everywhere." His hot gaze dropped to her mouth. "Especially here."

Then he dipped his head and kissed her, laughing softly when she gasped again. He ignored the invitation, sliding south to gently kiss her throat and the fluttering pulse at the base of her neck.

"You drive me crazy, do you know that?"

Oh, yeah. Crazy, she knew. Crazy she was feeling right now—especially with his warm mouth moving up her throat and sparking a prickly heat in her blood.

"G-good crazy?" she rasped, her hands coming up to clutch at his shoulders. "Or…b-bad?"

He sucked a patch of delicate skin into his mouth, drawing a ragged moan from her throat. "Bad," he murmured. "Very…*very*…bad."

A heavy lassitude invaded her limbs and she was tempted to slide right to the floor in a puddle of pleasure, but she locked her knees and demanded, "Is that good bad…or—"

"Good," he interrupted hoarsely. "Bad…but good. Definitely good." And before Paige could draw in another breath, he whipped her through the front door and backed her up against the interior wall. "So good," he continued as though he hadn't just scrambled her brains, "that I want to find out just…how…bad you…can be."

Breathless at the speed with which he'd moved, Paige gaped up at him, partly because *she* couldn't move—but mostly because he'd shoved a thigh between hers. He moved and the hem of her dress rose another couple of inches, causing the material of his jeans to scrape roughly against her inner thighs.

A good kind of rough—the kind that promptly sent a rush of liquid heat flooding her belly.

"What…what are you doing?" she squeaked, shocked more by the sensations flooding her than the fact that she was letting him manhandle her. Again.

Instead of replying, he nudged the door closed and pressed his muscled thigh closer to ground zero. And then…*oh, boy*…she experienced a rush to rival all rushes. Her head went light and her limbs heavy or she would have objected to what he did next.

Muttering something beneath his breath, his mouth came down on hers as a big warm hand slid up her thigh. The kiss was hot and hungry and just a little bit out of control, but the instant he cupped her bottom, she jolted.

"I...um... Ty?" She felt intoxicated—a little tipsy, a lot off balance—like she'd downed an entire bottle of red wine instead of just two glasses.

"You taste good," he murmured against her throat. "Like fruit..." Another inhalation. "Or... marshmallows."

"Cherries," she blurted out breathlessly. "It's... um...cherries." Maybe. Probably. She couldn't think, couldn't breathe and when his teeth gently raked the tendon in her throat, she lost all feeling in her legs. She would have slid to the floor except for the hard thigh between hers.

"You make me hungry," he growled, moving up her throat to nip at her chin and swipe his tongue along her bottom lip.

His fingers squeezed her bottom and a desperate pulsing began deep in her belly. She shuddered. "I...uh...you've just eaten."

His chuckle was soft and deep. "Not that kind of hunger," he murmured, tracing an invisible line of fire from the corner of her mouth to her ear with his tongue. "The kind that's been driving me crazy since...the night...you...decorated...me in pink." Each word or phrase was accompanied by a nip with his sharp white teeth. "But things are about to change."

She heard a moan. Probably hers. "They…are?"

"Oh, yeah." Ty murmured something that sounded a lot like, "And I'm going to start right here." Then his hand slid beneath her panties to squeeze her naked bottom and Paige nearly shot through the roof. Suddenly, any thoughts of resisting—*yeah, right*—faded and all she could concentrate on were the sensations invading her body.

A whimper escaped that might have embarrassed her if she'd been able to think clearly.

She wasn't. She could only feel.

And, boy, there was suddenly a heck of a lot *to* feel. His chest, his hands, his mouth…his belly— oh, God—those rock-hard abs and thighs…*everything* between. Every…long…thick…hard…inch.

He growled and the sound stuck her as thrilling and unbearably exciting. Breathing heavily, Ty lifted his head.

"Say it."

"Uh… I… What?"

"Say it."

"This is a b-bad idea?"

"The very worst," he murmured agreeably. So

agreeably that she pulled back and tried to shove him off her but he simply pressed closer, cupping the back of her head in his big palm and brushing his mouth across her cheekbone, her mouth... her chin...her neck. In fact, everywhere he could reach. Barely-there caresses that made her shudder and lose her train of thought.

He must have felt it too because his mouth caught hers and suddenly he was devouring it like he'd been starved of oxygen and wanted to gulp it all in at once. Fill his lungs...fill himself with her.

"Paige," he rasped, sucking in air like a drowning victim. "If you're going to stop...do it...now. Before I—"

"Don't," she growled fiercely, arching into his gently grinding movements. "Don't...you... dare...stop or...or I'll... *Oh*..." She was unravelling faster than she could drag air into her lungs. "If you stop, I...promise..." another breathy moan followed by a growl "... I'll... I'll hurt you."

His chuckle was as rough and ragged as her breathing. "Oh, yeah?" he said, teasing her with sharp little nips to her shoulder. "How bad can it be, Dr. Cutie?"

"Three brothers," she reminded him, turning

her head to nip at his jaw in punishment. "They taught me to fight...dirty."

He stilled and after a couple of beats leaned back to look into her face. Eyes, hot and heavy, glittered beneath the slash of his dark brows.

"How dirty?" he demanded, looking dubious and hopeful at the same time.

Her slow smile was filled with reckless mischief. "Very...*very* dirty," she promised, and launched herself at him.

Stunned by the suddenness of her move, Ty stumbled back a few steps, barely catching her before she thudded against him. And before he could draw in his next ragged breath she wrapped her slender legs around his hips, grabbed his hair and yanked his mouth to hers.

Ty staggered backwards under the assault. His knees were as steady as cooked noodles and he felt drunk, as if he'd spent all weekend on a bender. But that was probably because she was sucking the air from his lungs and rubbing against his erection like she couldn't get enough.

"Wait..." he rasped, seeing stars and weaving like a drunken reveler at Mardi Gras. "God... *wait!*" They stumbled into the entrance table, knocking over the flashlight. Paige snorted a laugh against his mouth and clenched her thigh muscles, the move killing off a few more trillion brain cells.

He muttered a curse under his breath and changed direction, heading for the living room, needing to get them horizontal before he lost all feeling in his legs.

Paige refused to co-operate, sliding her tongue against his and then giggling like a loon when they bumped into the wall, the archway and then a side table. A lamp went crashing to the floor and he lurched sideways. The next instant they tumbled onto the couch in a tangle of limbs.

For long tense moments neither of them moved except for their ragged breathing. It took him a few extra beats to realize that Paige was shaking, her whole body trembling.

Aw, man. Had he hurt her? He'd meant to twist so that she landed on him...not the other way around.

"Paige," he said, gently running a trembling hand down the elegant line of her spine. She was small, delicate and sweet...and gasping like he'd crushed her chest. "Paige..." he rasped, "you... okay?"

Then she gave a muffled snort and tried to bite him and Ty finally caught on. He fisted a hand in her hair and yanked her up and—yep, just as he'd thought.

He stared at her. Okay. Not so sweet.

"You're laughing?"

She gave another strangled snort and he dropped his head back, huffing out a laughing curse that had her giggling even louder. Then she tried to sort out their tangled limbs, managing somehow to shove her elbow in his trachea and knee him in the nuts.

"Holy hell, woman," he growled through the roaring in his head. "Watch where you put that knee."

He tried to grab her leg but his casted hand couldn't get a grip. Finally, with much fumbling and giggling, she got her knees under her and sat up, straddling his hips, all flushed and tousled and glowing with triumph.

He blinked up at her, breath working its way in and out of his lungs like bellows. And then he promptly lost it again when he *really* looked at her—hair tousled, mouth red and slick and swollen from his kisses.

Her eyes sparkled with mirth and...yeah, arousal.

No mistaking that. His heart gave a vicious kick against his ribs and he stilled, gazing up at her because, in that moment—flushed, half-naked and her face alight with laughter—he'd never seen anyone more beautiful.

For long moments they stared at each other. Something about his confused emotions must have shown on his face because her laughter faded and her eyes darkened uncertainly.

"If this is where you tell me that this is temporary and you're leaving soon, I know," she said, suddenly dead serious. "It's okay. In fact, it's great…really great, because…because that's all I'm offering too. This…" she gestured wildly, nearly whacking him in the face "…is it. A one-night-only offer."

Feeling both relieved and irritated, Ty caught her hand before she hurt herself or broke his nose. "That's not what I was going to say," he growled. "But I'm glad you said one night and not one time. Because, Dr. Carlyle, once won't be nearly enough."

Her brow rose. "Sounds like a challenge, Dr. Reese."

Even as his hands slid from her knees to her

hips, pulling her in hard, Ty was shaking his head. "Not...a...challenge," he rasped. "A...promise."

Damn...she felt good. Better than good. Especially when she uttered a laughing gasp and placed her lips on his throat. Her tongue flicked out, and fire flashed across his skin, eliciting a deep groan. She lifted her head to gloat and he gently wrapped a hand around her neck, catching her mouth to launch his own assault.

Within seconds she was making those sexy sounds that threatened to blow his mind and she slid her soft palms down his chest to his zipper to press against his erection.

He felt his eyes roll back in his head. Her mouth curved and with her stormy eyes locked on him, she slowly straightened and...popped the button.

The whirr of his zipper was drowned by her appreciative hum and the next instant her hand slid into his opened jeans to wrap around his length. He gave an involuntary moan.

"You like?" she purred, nipping at his lip and setting off a series of shudders that licked at his spine like fire.

"Oh, yeah," he croaked, wondering if he would be forced to turn in his man-card if he begged. And, *man*, he was close, very close to begging.

It took Ty less than five seconds to get naked, whipping around when she gasped.

"Omigod," she squeaked. "You're huge."

Rolling his eyes, he huffed out a ragged laugh. "I'm not *that* big, Paige." Then, abruptly realizing he'd just insulted himself, he quickly amended, "Okay, I am, but I'll go slowly. I promise."

With a wicked grin and a low appreciative sound, he lifted his hands to her breasts, brushing the backs of his fingers against the tight buds clearly visible through her dress. Her back arched and her head fell back, her eyes slowly drifting closed.

Her sigh sent an unnamed emotion slicing through to his chest to lodge right next to his heart. It felt a bit like heartburn but seemed an awful lot like affection and something much more dangerous…something he didn't dare name.

Desperate to ignore it, he surged up and whipped Paige's dress over her head. Her bra followed and, wrapping an arm around her, he flipped her over so he was kneeling between her splayed thighs.

Then he tugged her panties down her slender legs and tossed them over his shoulder before she could protest. And suddenly he couldn't breathe because she was finally beneath him, naked and flushed, looking like a sensual feast when he had no idea what to sample first.

"Don't...don't look at me like that."

He lifted his head and caught her biting her lip. Okay, so he did know where to start. He'd start at her mouth and work his way down to paradise.

Carefully balancing his weight on one elbow, he lowered his body over hers, groaning when her warm silky skin slid against his.

"Like what?" he murmured against her throat.

She turned her head, silently inviting his mouth to feast on her tender flesh. "Like you...want to, um..." ended on a sigh as though she'd forgotten what she wanted to say.

"Take a couple of hundred greedy bites out of you?"

"Yes...that." She sounded distracted, humming in the back of her throat as her hands explored his shoulders, his back and his butt. As though she needed to touch all of him at once.

He drew back far enough to see her eyes, soft and clouded with desire. Realizing he was studying her; she tried to cover herself.

"Nuh-uh." He laughed softly, catching her hands. "No hiding."

He stroked his hand up her belly to cup her

breasts, thumbing her velvety areolas and watching in fascination as they tightened.

"Ty…" she choked out, squirming against him until he bent his head and took one nipple in his mouth, his hand skimming south, between her legs. *"Omigod,"* she whimpered when his thumb bumped against her little knot of nerve endings. It had her undulating into his strokes with growing urgency.

He'd been watching his hands explore her but at her gasp his gaze flew up and he couldn't look away. Her eyes drifted closed as he slid a finger between her tight folds, a flush of arousal staining her lightly tanned skin a deep beguiling rose. It was the hottest thing he'd ever seen.

He must have touched a particularly sensitive spot because her body spasmed and her eyes flew open, dazed and dark with arousal.

"Oh… I…" she breathed, and just when he thought it too much too soon, she moaned and parted her legs. Her hands rose to clutch his biceps as though she was afraid he might stop.

"Tell me."

"I…uh…" She gave an inarticulate little cry, bucking, straining against him when he added another finger.

He could feel her trembling on the edge and again ordered, "Tell me," as his thumb slowly circled the knot of nerves at her center.

Strung as tight as a bow, she breathlessly demanded, "*Omigod*, you want to talk *now*?"

"Tell me you want me and I'll give you what you need."

"I…want… I…*you*," she managed, her head tossing from side to side as she made soft huffing sounds, her face a mask of agonized pleasure.

"Good enough." He chuckled, keeping her balanced on the edge several moments more before finally giving her what she needed—an orgasm that took her apart as completely as it took her by surprise.

Her eyes flew open and locked on his as she shattered and it was the sweetest, most erotic thing he'd witnessed.

Finally, she collapsed beneath him, her eyes drifting shut on a ragged sigh. Quickly retrieving the condom from his jeans pocket, Ty rolled it down his shaft and then, lacing his fingers with hers, he lowered himself between her quivering thighs.

The moment his erection bumped against her damp flesh, Ty saw stars. He gritted his teeth against the urge to thrust home and find release but he wanted to see her eyes go all misty with pleasure when she climaxed again.

"Again," he rasped.

She gave a ragged, breathless laugh and clutched at him. "I… I can't," she gasped, whimpering and squirming until he pinned her hips, rocking… rocking against her as he stared into her dazed expression.

The sight of her deepening flush was enough to make Ty go a little crazy then. His hand smoothed the length of her thigh, his long-fingered surgeon's hand detecting the fine quivers rippling just beneath her skin. Then he wrapped his hand around the back of her knee and gently lifted.

Positioning himself, he slowly pushed into her, groaning when her tight flesh clamped down on him. She immediately wrapped her legs and arms around him and bucked. Once. Twice.

Gritting his teeth for control, Ty sucked in a ragged breath and began to move. Slowly. He wanted it to build, to savor the incredible sensations, but Paige had other ideas. She gave an impatient growl and reared up, sinking her teeth into his shoulder. The unexpectedness of it jolted him and they fell off the couch, Paige landing on him with a surprised *"Oomph"*.

After a startled pause, she gave a muffled giggle that ended in a long low groan when Ty rolled them across the floor and thrust deep. Then he stilled, dropping his face into her neck to keep from having a brain explosion. Or maybe another kind of explosion. One that threatened to streak up his spine like a bolt of lightning and fry all his neuro-circuits.

Paige's breath hitched and she brought up her knees to hug his hips and score her nails down his spine. It was the impetus his body needed and before he knew it he was pulling out and shoving in deep, over and over again as he raced for the finish.

Gasping out a triumphant laugh, she threw back her head, looking so gorgeous and hot that he lost his legendary control. In seconds her body began to ripple around his and he watched, fascinated, as her eyes went blind. A wild flush rose beneath her skin and in the next instant she arched up and came, a long low moan torn from her throat.

The sight—and sounds—of her pleasure triggered his own and with a hoarse bellow he followed her over the edge.

CHAPTER EIGHT

IT WAS JUST before six when Paige pulled into the hospital staff parking. Her shift didn't start until seven but apparently good—*okay, spectacular*—sex gave her a massive burst of energy that left her tingling all over and raring to start the day.

Or maybe it was the full-blown freak-out she'd been heading for ever since she'd awakened wrapped in delicious heat and Ty's amazing man scent. Just the sight of him, sprawled face down across her bed, gloriously and edibly naked, had given her such a rush that she'd been tempted to jump his bones. Again.

Fortunately the cool bathroom air had cleared her head of all the intoxicating pheromones temporarily rendering her stupid.

Standing on the cold tiles, getting her breathing under control, it had seemed like a good idea to head into work early to avoid any awkward morning-after moments.

She sighed. Okay, so she'd panicked and run. *Big deal.*

It was over; she could finally get on with her life without obsessing about the sexy guy next door: *blah-blah-blah.* Besides, Ty wasn't the kind of man to get stupid over someone like her and wanting more was just...*stupid, okay.* It was stupid. She got that.

Yeesh.

He was just one of those hot temporary flings every woman deserved to experience at least once in her life. At the advanced age of thirty she'd finally done it. *Yay.*

Just then she caught sight of her reflection in the rear-view mirror and did a double take. *Yikes.* She was wearing a sappy grin that just screamed... *Paige Carlyle Got Lucky Last Night.* And that wouldn't do. So she promptly scowled to erase all evidence—along with memories—of the past eight hours.

See, she told her reflection smugly. *Easy as that.*

Mood lifting at the very adult way she was handling things, Paige got out and stretched all those aching muscles she'd forgotten she had. It also made her realize how hungry she was.

In fact, she was starving. So, instead of heading

for ER, she walked through the automatic doors and hurried down the passage to the cafeteria. It was still early and the tables were mostly empty.

Grabbing a tray, Paige ordered coffee, a couple of pastries and then, because her breakfast looked unhealthy, added an apple just as her phone buzzed.

It was a text from "kick-ass grl". Turn around, it said, and when Paige turned, she saw Frankie holding up the far wall, booted feet propped on the chair beside her.

Paige quickly paid for her breakfast and headed over.

"How was your date?" Frankie asked casually the instant Paige got close. "The one I had to find out about from the waitress at Surf 'n Turf, by the way, because my *best friend* doesn't tell me anything."

Paige shrugged casually, hoping her expression didn't give her away. "It was more like a...favor."

She mentally rolled her eyes at the lie.

"Right," Frankie drawled. "A favor. Like having dinner with a sexy surgeon on vacation is a favor." She snorted and waggled her eyebrows. "So did he do *you* any...um...favors?"

"What? *No!*" Paige spluttered in protest, covering her pink face by sliding into the opposite chair. She glared at her friend. "Get your mind out of the gutter, will you? It was a mutual *dinner* favor. My refrigerator was empty and he... well, he needed someone to have dinner with so people wouldn't feel sorry for him."

Frankie snorted her opinion of anyone feeling sorry for Ty Reese. "And after?"

"After?" Paige asked innocently, reaching for a stick of sugar. "What after?"

Out the corner of her eye she caught Frankie's narrow-eyed scrutiny and tried not to look as guilty as she felt. After a short pause the other woman's eyes widened and her feet hit the floor with a loud thud. "You did it, didn't you?" she accused. "You finally did it."

Startled, Paige paused in the process of dumping sugar in her coffee. "Did what? What did I do?"

"Not what," Frankie snorted, pointing her finger reproachfully at Paige. "Who."

Heat climbed into her face and Paige grabbed the to-go coffee to hide behind. "I have absolutely no idea what you're talking about."

Reaching across the table, Frankie nudged

Paige's hand down and snorted. "Oh, yes, you do." Her eyes sparkled with laughter. "You did Ty."

Gasping, Paige made an attempt to shush her but Frankie smirked and chortled, "And by the look on your face, spectacularly too."

Paige hissed at her to be quiet and darted a guilty look around at the other patrons. "Dammit," she muttered, turning back with a scowl only to find Frankie grinning like a loon.

"So-o-o-o-o," her friend said, drawing out the single word into about a million syllables. "Spill everything, Dr. Cutie. I need details."

Paige scowled. "What are we, twelve?"

"Of course not." Frankie snickered, looking cool and sophisticated even in her paramedic jumpsuit. "Not unless twelve-year-olds are having spectacular sex with hot surgeons. Besides," she continued, clearly enjoying Paige's discomfort, "it's about time you did something stupid."

"What?" *Did Frankie read minds now too?*

"Yep. Because getting involved with Ty?" She shook her head. "Stupid."

"Who said anything about getting involved?" Paige muttered irritably. "Besides, I told you it wasn't a date." Her face grew hot at Frankie's derisive snort. "And how the heck can you tell, anyway?" she demanded huffily. "It's not like I'm wearing a neon sign that says 'Paige Carlyle got some last night'."

Frankie's brow arched. "Maybe it's the hickey on your neck and the deer-in-the-headlights look."

Paige slapped one hand to her neck and the other to her eyes. "I do not!" she gasped, horrified that despite her efforts to appear as though everything was fine...it apparently wasn't even close.

Frankie reached into her shoulder bag and withdrew a compact mirror. "You most certainly do," she drawled, grinning when Paige grabbed for it. "You were also wearing a sappy grin when you walked in and no one smiles at the crack of dawn unless they got lucky."

Horrified, Paige fumbled the compact and finally got it open. Fortunately there was no sappy grin, but there *was* a hickey—no, two *dammit*. And then—*Omigod!*—she saw a third, on the upper curve of her breast when she pulled at the neck of her T-shirt.

"I do," she gasped, trying unsuccessfully to cover the damning evidence. "I totally do. I look like a..." She gulped and snapped her mouth closed.

Frankie leaned closer and prompted, "You look like a what?"

"Like a starved woman," Paige said firmly, grabbing a pastry and shoving it in her mouth. She was absolutely *not* going to discuss how she looked in case she started freaking out again.

"Satisfied and pretty darned smug, you mean." Frankie chortled. "If I wasn't so envious, I'd say good for you." Paige made a sound of distress and after a couple of beats Frankie leaned forward, all signs of amusement gone. "I hope you know what you're doing, Paige," she said quietly. "Ty is…"

She swallowed the pastry without tasting it. "Bad. Yep, got that." *But so* good *at being bad.* She hadn't thought she'd prefer Frankie's teasing but the sudden turn the conversation was taking had turned her stomach to lead because the truth was…she *didn't* know what she was doing.

Oh, boy.

She'd thought she could easily handle a casual fling, but she was beginning to suspect that she wasn't wired that way. It might have something to do with her childhood, but Paige tended to want the impossible. She wanted permanence and Ty… well, he was the last thing in permanence. She knew that.

She really did.

"He'll leave and—"

"Break my heart. Yes I *know*."

Frankie's expression was a mix of affection, exasperation and concern. "I just don't want to see you hurt," Frankie said quietly.

"I'm not going to get hurt, Frankie," Paige sighed, reaching over to squeeze her friend's hand. "I know what I'm doing. Really."

But Paige didn't know what she was doing and it was all Tyler Reese's fault. *Damn him.* With his deep bedroom voice...and sexy blue eyes...and hot, hard body...

Oh, my lord, Paige thought in dismay. *I'm in trouble. Big, bad, sexy trouble.*

Ty woke to the sound of banging and for several moments he wondered where he was. That was until he'd got a whiff of Paige's seductive scent and went instantly hard when memories of the past eight hours flooded back in a rush of images.

He rolled over but even before his hand slid to the spot where he'd last seen her, he'd known he was alone. And some idiot was banging on the front door.

Grabbing a towel from the bathroom, he stomped

down the stairs and yanked open the front door with a snarl on his lips.

Nate leaned against the wall, looking cool and wide awake as he studied Ty over the top of his aviator shades.

"What?" was Ty's surly demand to the other man's arched brow. He hadn't had much sleep but should've been relaxed after all the physical activity of the night before. Waking up alone hadn't been nearly the relief he'd thought it would be. In fact, he was feeling like a one-night stand—only in reverse because he was usually the one to bail before morning.

"Good morning to you too," Nate said holding up a food bag and a tray of to-go coffee.

Ty scrubbed a hand down his face and demanded, "What are you doing here?"

"I'm here to save you from the big bad Navy SEAL that was waiting on your doorstep, looking like he was ready to use his government-trained assassin skills."

Ty looked around. "What SEAL?"

"Hey," Nate said, sounding insulted. Probably because he thought he was big and bad. "I was actually talking about the one looking for his sister." He offered Ty a large covered disposable coffee cup before adding, "Dr. Paige Carlyle. I can just imagine his reaction at finding some naked dude answering her door."

Nate laughed at the look on Ty's face and Ty folded his arms across his chest and spent the next few moments rethinking his views on physical violence.

"You should see the look on your face." Nate snickered, clearly enjoying Ty's predicament.

"I'm tempted to wipe that smirk off yours," Ty growled, wiping his hand down his face. "But I've just had surgery."

"Like you could," Nate finally managed. "Relax, T. I sent him to the hospital. To see his sister." He grinned when Ty's eyes widened. "A good thing too or he'd have made mincemeat of you."

Ty wanted to say he could take care of himself, but his hand was in a cast and he didn't think his shoulder would withstand a Navy SEAL attack. Especially after discovering Ty had slept with his sister.

"What are you doing here?" he asked instead. "I thought you were working."

Nate shrugged. "One of the guys wanted to trade days, so I thought we could go sailing. I knocked at your door *and* called your phone but you didn't answer. So I decided to try here." He chuckled. "*After* I sent the SEAL away. Imagine my surprise when you actually opened the door, because the last time I asked, you said she was a pain in the ass. You were here because you needed peace and quiet and didn't need any annoying distractions. No matter how cute they were."

Ignoring him, Ty looked up at the sky. It was clear, but in typical Pacific North West spring fashion, the wind coming off the strait was freezing.

Dressed in only a towel, *he* was freezing.

"You want to go sailing? In this weather?"

Nate looked out at the morning and turned back with a raised brow. "What's the matter? It's a perfect day for sailing. If you're too much of a California wuss to handle a little fresh breeze, I totally understand."

With a growl, Ty pulled Nate inside. "Get in here, *dammit*. Before the neighbors call the cops."

"Yeah," Nate drawled, stepping over the threshold. "I can see why they would."

Pausing in the process of shutting the door, Ty demanded, "What's that supposed to mean?"

"It means there's a naked man in Dr. Cutie's house again." He pulled off his shades. "Why exactly are you in the cute doctor's house instead of next door? Where you have a perfectly good shower of your own?"

Ty slammed the door and turned, almost colliding with Nate, who'd stopped dead. "Never mind." The other man chuckled, catching sight of the bits of clothing scattered across the entrance floor. "I can totally see what happened."

Ty shoved him aside and bent to gather up the discarded clothing. "Yeah?" Ty demanded. "Maybe she had intruders last night who left a mess. Ever think of that?"

Snickering rudely, Nate hooked his shades in the neck of his T. "What I think is that you clearly have a thing for Dr. Cutie. If I'd known, I would have introduced you to her brother. You know, meet the family and all."

"I don't have a 'thing' for anyone and she doesn't like to be called cute," Ty snarled irritably, beginning to pull on his clothes. And he was *not* meeting Paige's family, for God's sake. *Jeez Louise*, they'd only known each other a few weeks and most of that time he'd managed to avoid her.

He most definitely did not have a "thing" for her. Or anyone else, for that matter.

He found a teeny little pair of baby-blue panties

covered with white daisies and shoved them in his pocket because Paige didn't need Nate looking at her underwear.

"We're not a thing." Nate's expression was a mix of pity and amusement. "What?"

His friend shook his head. "You poor stupid sap. Look at you defending your lady and hiding her skivvies from your best friend."

"She's not my lady," Ty denied quickly, and then winced at the knee-jerk response. And because he felt guilty he growled, "And you're no longer my best friend."

Nate looked unconcerned. "Then you won't mind if I ask her out, because word is she's a lot of fun."

It took a couple of beats for Ty to process that but when he did, he rounded on Nate with a protesting snarl.

His ex-friend merely snorted. "Yeah, thought so," he drawled. "You so have a thing for the cute doctor. Relax. The guys say that, as fun as she is, *they* don't get to see her skivvies." Ty's shoulders tensed at the news that the coasties were discussing Paige. He was about to point out that Nate was gossiping like a little girl when his friend added,

"Guess they'll be interested to know she wears teeny blue ones covered with little white daisies."

In the process of pulling his shirt over his head, Ty's head snapped up to find his friend looking enormously entertained at his expense. "You do that," he told Nate, "and I'll kick your ass all the way to Canada and back."

Instead of answering, the other man simply grinned and dumped the bag of food onto the entrance table while Ty finished yanking on his clothes.

It was only when they were on the boat, heading out into open water, that Nate called out as he steered into a large swell, "So, if Dr. Cutie isn't your lady, what is she?"

Ty pretended not to hear. Besides, he didn't know what Paige was other than sweet and sexy... oh, yeah, and hot. She was also smart and funny and surprisingly vulnerable beneath that sassy tough-girl exterior. And just thinking about how she looked when she came had him fumbling the ropes and cursing.

She wasn't his lady, he insisted silently. She'd made that abundantly clear by sneaking out without saying goodbye. Yet *something*—he didn't know what—wanted more than one night. More than— *No, dammit,* he snarled silently. *I don't want or need anything from—*

"Look out!"

He looked up as the boom swung at his head, and ducked just in time to avoid being dumped into the icy ocean. He straightened and a voice in the back of his head warned, *Excellent advice, buddy. You'd be smart to heed it.*

When Paige knocked off work a few days later, clouds, dark and heavy, lashed the seaside town with rain while high seas pounded the shore.

Within seconds she was soaked and had to go scrambling around in the rising water to retrieve her keys, which had slipped from her cold fingers. When she finally got her car open, she sat shivering and dripping all over the interior, wondering if she should stay put or risk the drive home.

As promised, Harry had negotiated a good deal that hadn't resulted in her selling a kidney or wiping out her savings; but the mechanic had warned Paige to be careful about driving in wet conditions until the engine had been completely overhauled.

She rolled her eyes. *Yeah, right.* She'd put it on her list right after the entry that said: *Stop thinking about you know who.*

Deciding to leave the decision up to Bertha, she turned the key and exhaled gustily when the engine turned over.

"Okay," she muttered. "Home it is, then."

The streets were deserted. Water gushed across the roads, turning them into fast-flowing rivers, and she was forced to grip the steering wheel when Bertha abruptly hydroplaned across an intersection. Now, instead of shivering with cold, she was shaking with terror and sucking in air like a vacuum cleaner.

She was halfway home when rain turned to sleet, pinging against her roof like tiny missiles that turned her windshield to slush and the road to an ice rink. By the time she parked in front of her house she was a wreck.

She hurried up the path to her front door on wobbly legs, only to discover that everything was in darkness. Clutching her shoulder bag as ice dripped off her nose, Paige fished out her house keys with stiff fingers…and sneaked a peek at the adjacent unit before she could stop herself.

She hadn't seen Ty since "The Night", as she'd dubbed it, and considering it would take her about a decade, maybe longer, to forget the way she'd thrown herself at him, she was quite happy to keep it that way.

She didn't know what she'd expected but it wasn't seeing the front door standing wide open. *What the heck?* She paused. Surely he hadn't just walked out and forgotten to lock up? Or maybe he couldn't because something bad had happened.

Hurrying across the space separating their front doors, Paige peered around the frame, half expecting someone to leap out and scare the bejesus out of her. When nothing happened, she sucked in an unsteady breath and ventured inside.

Dim light from the marina made its way through the sitting room sliding doors but other than a lot of dark shapes Paige hoped were just pieces of furniture, the place was empty.

Maybe. Hopefully.

"Ty?" she called, moving to the bottom of the stairs that led to the second floor. "Tyler?"

Not wanting to be like the brainless bimbo in a slasher movie, Paige retraced her steps thinking that maybe Ty had gone to check on the connection box. In that moment her worst nightmare—and all those horror movies she'd watched with Frankie—materialized as a huge hulking shadow, backlit by a raging storm, appeared in the doorway.

Paige opened her mouth to scream and a deep familiar voice demanded, "What the—? Paige?"

She gave a strangled gasp and lurched backwards. It was only when her butt hit the floor that she realized her legs had given way.

The next thing Ty was crouched over her. "Paige," he demanded, reaching out to tuck dripping black strands behind her ear, "what the hell happened? Answer me, *dammit*. Where are you hurt?"

No way was she saying her butt. That would be mortifying, especially if he demanded to examine it. "Just p-peachy," she finally gasped, her breath hitching on a giggle that bordered on hysteria. *Great*. Looking like a drowned, terrified rat was so *not* how she'd imagined their next meeting. "Y-you," she babbled, wrapping her arms around her knees because she was suddenly shaking like she had dengue fever.

"Yeah. Me." He frowned and wrapped his fingers around her wrist to check her pulse. When she continued to giggle helplessly he nudged her chin up to peer into her face.

The next instant his searching blue gaze had her trembling for another reason entirely. One that was as unwelcome as it was unsettling. For some reason she sat, frozen by the expression in his eyes, the heat pumping off his body and…and the memory of— *Nope. So not going there.*

"I'm fine," she insisted, shoving his hand away and scrambling to her feet. She wrapped her arms around her body and edged away. "I'll just… I saw your d-door open and thought…uh, never mind." What she'd thought was ridiculous so she headed for the door, her teeth chattering from a combination of cold and reaction.

"Hey, wait up. Where are you going?"

"Since you're okay, I'll… I'll… I need to go." *Far away.* From the delicious heat pumping off his body and the dreams that had plagued her the past couple nights. Just thinking about them gave her a hot flash.

"Don't be ridiculous," he growled, pulling her back around and clearly having no problem facing *her*. But then he probably did this all the time, she thought darkly.

"There's no power. I was trying to fix the problem at the outside box but I can't see what the hell I'm doing." He disappeared for a minute and returned with a couple of towels. "This storm literally came out of nowhere," he continued, running one towel over his hair and holding out the other.

She took it and immediately buried her face in the thick terry cloth. "Just before the power went out the radio said the storm's being driven by the collision of a warm front from California and a huge polar cell pushing its way south."

Paige peered out into the icy storm and shivered as the wind sent sleet angling in under the porch roof. The only way she could make out the houses across the street was from the faint glow of lights through the gloom.

Moving to the end of the porch, she looked around the side of the house. Marina lights swung crazily in the gusting winds, and Paige could scarcely see the boats and yachts lurching around at their slips. What she couldn't see was Harry's lights.

"Are we the only ones without power?"

She leaned out further and would have taken off in the wind if Ty hadn't grabbed the back of her scrubs and hauled her back.

"Get back from there before you get soaked," he growled. "And I think so. Although…now that you mention it I think the Andersen house was in darkness. Is Harry away somewhere? Or is their house also on this circuit?"

Really worried now, Paige nibbled on her

thumbnail. "I'm going to check on him," she announced, a bad feeling cramping her belly.

"I'll go," Ty began, but Paige shoved the towel at him and hurried down the stairs. She heard him curse and mutter something about stubborn females as she ran into the street. She barely felt the additional moisture, only swiping irritably at the bits of sleet dripping into her eyes as she raised a hand to knock on Harry's door.

By the time she realized no one was going to answer, Ty was a large comforting presence beside her, trying the handle while she peered in through the panes beside the door.

"Don't panic," he said gruffly. "I'm sure he's okay. Maybe he fell asleep in front of the TV."

"It's not like him," she murmured, her stomach cramping again at the thought of something happening to the old man. In the eight months he'd been her neighbor she'd come to love the retired widower like a grandfather.

She couldn't bear it if anything happened to him.

Shaking now from more than cold, Paige hurried round the house to the stairs leading to the deck. The wood was slick with ice and she nearly took a header into Harry's window box.

Pushing open the sliding door with shaking hands, she was both relieved and frightened when she found it unlocked and the house dark and silent.

"Harry? Mr. Andersen, it's Paige. Are you okay?" Please be okay, she prayed frantically, hoping he'd be sitting in his chair, startled out of sleep.

What she found had her heart squeezing in her chest. "Harry?" She rushed over to where he lay in a heap on the floor, dropping to her knees beside him. "Harry, can you hear me?"

CHAPTER NINE

"BE CAREFUL," TY WARNED, coming up behind her. "Don't turn him over until you know what you're dealing with. I'll call emergency and unlock the front door."

She nodded, unable to talk past the huge lump in her throat as she slid her fingers beneath Harry's jaw. She found a pulse and went weak with relief. Thank God. He was alive, although his pulse was way too fast and all over the place.

"He's alive," she called out, and heard Ty murmur something. When he reappeared in the doorway, she continued, "I've got a pulse but he's in A fib with brief periods of PSVT. I'm going to turn him over and start compressions. How long till the EMTs get here?"

His face was set in unreadable lines. "We're on our own," he said, dropping to his haunches and helping roll the old man onto his back. "There's been a pile-up on the highway so they may take a while."

Paige's heart squeezed at the news. Even in the torchlight, she could see the ashen tinge to Harry's weather-toughened skin. Her hands shook as she checked his pupil reaction. She'd never had to perform emergency procedures on someone she knew or loved.

She placed the heel of her bottom hand on Harry's sternum and laced her fingers. "How long?"

"Ten...fifteen minutes...an hour...they can't tell." Her heart dropped. Ty must have seen something in her face because he reached out and placed a hand over hers. It was warm and firm and she had to fight against the urge to cling to it. But clinging meant you expected the person to always be there and Paige had learned early that was never the case.

"Just keep doing what you're doing," Ty said. "Where's your emergency kit?"

Without breaking rhythm, she lifted her head and their eyes caught and held. His were steady and calm.

"In the upstairs spare bedroom. My keys are—"

But Ty was already gone and by the time he returned she'd had time to examine Harry more carefully in the torchlight. All the signs pointed to dehydration. Low electrolytes could easily have triggered atrial fibrillation, especially if he had an underlying condition. She wasn't certain what had caused him to lose consciousness but the first order of business was to get a sinus rhythm back.

They could deal with everything else later.

Sucking in a shaky breath, Paige sent up a prayer that the AMTs arrived in time to help him. She couldn't...just couldn't bear to lose him too. Not now.

He'd need a calcium channel blocker and her main worry was blood pooling in his heart. If it began clotting, he could die before they got him to the ER.

Within minutes Ty was back, tossing a package at her.

"Find a vein," he instructed tersely, pulling out a bag of Ringer's lactate. "He needs liquids ASAP. I found some anti-diarrhea meds on the counter. Probably caught the enterovirus going around and tried to treat it himself."

That sounded like Harry, but Paige blamed herself for not keeping closer tabs on him. She'd been so preoccupied with avoiding Ty and pretending her life wasn't unravelling like a pair of cheap pantyhose that she'd barely been home or even thought to check on Harry the past week.

And now he could die.

Hands shaking, she tried to find a vein, finally applying a tourniquet and quickly inserting the needle when one appeared. She attached the cannula and slapped an adhesive dressing over the area to stabilize it while Ty awkwardly hooked the bag one-handed to the back of the chair.

"No CCBs," he said gruffly, rising to his feet to look around the kitchen. "Without channel blockers we need some electrolytes."

"Try the cupboards," Paige suggested, resuming chest compressions. "I know Epsom salts isn't ideal but he uses them for his plants. We need some dextrose too so check the cupboard beside the stove. Maybe there's something there or in the bathroom that we can use."

Ty rummaged around in the cupboards, grunting with disappointment each time he found nothing. He finally headed off to the bathroom, calling out a minute later that he'd found something.

Paige flashed a nervous look at the kitchen clock, wondering how long Harry had been unconscious. They'd been there nearly seven minutes already and still no sign of the EMTs.

Ty reappeared, holding a container, and went straight to the kitchen cupboard. He took out a cup and rinsed it with water from the kettle before dumping contents from the container into the cup. He added a few drops of kettle water and reached into the overhead cabinet for a bottle of honey.

He added a drop to the mixture and gently mixed it.

"Mag chloride and five percent glucose," he growled. "We'll repeat it every half-hour till the EMTs get here." He thrust the cup at her. "I'll take over compressions while you inject this into the line."

"Ty…" With his cast he wouldn't be able to perform CPR properly.

"I can't handle a syringe one-handed," he snapped, and Paige took the cup from him. "I can't do a damn thing one-handed."

She couldn't help noticing that he'd once again retreated behind an invisible wall, just as he had that afternoon on the mountain.

It felt like an age since she'd overheard him telling Nate that he might not be able to resume his surgical career. But even if that was true, he could still consult in other ways…especially with all his medical knowledge and skill. He couldn't just waste it—people needed him.

"You're more than a surgeon," she said abruptly,

and when he looked up, she nearly bobbled the cup at his shuttered expression and chilly eyes, as if she was a stranger who'd overstepped her mark. A muscle flexed in his jaw and the tension in the room ratcheted skyward until he turned away.

Okay. Clearly that was an unwelcome subject.

Furious with herself for getting all girly and hurt like they were an item, she turned her back on him and concentrated on getting the solution into a syringe. Harry she could help, Ty, it seemed… not so much.

She injected the solution right into the cannula port and altered the flow rate then dropped to her haunches. She made to take over but Ty brushed her aside with a brusque, "Call again."

Grinding her teeth together, she rose and snatched his cell off the table. "I didn't ask," she reminded him furiously. "You could just as easily have gone on ignoring everyone and everything the way you like. Besides, you came here to be alone, remember? I didn't ask for anything from you."

Without looking at her, he said coolly, "No. You wouldn't, would you?"

Stunned by the accusation, she demanded, "What's that supposed to mean?"

"It means that Paige Carlyle likes everyone to believe she can handle things just fine on her own."

She opened her mouth to tell him that she'd been forced to handle everything from the age of fifteen when she heard a siren. She snapped her mouth closed and rushed to open the front door just as her friend dashed up the stairs.

Frankie's partner, Dale Franklin, followed with a covered stretcher, grunting his thanks when Paige helped him haul it onto the porch. They heard Frankie demanding, "What happened? How bad is it? And— what the hell, Ty?"

Paige had the feeling the last question didn't have a thing to do with Harry and hurried back to stop Frankie from interrogating Ty about "The Night". His murmured response was drowned out by the sound of Dale's footsteps thudding down the passage behind her and by the time they entered, Frankie was checking Harry's BP and ignoring Ty.

He had his hip propped against the counter, arms folded across his wide chest, when Paige returned. His mouth was pressed into a firm, unsmiling line that made her think he hadn't liked Frankie's questions. With his hooded gaze on

Paige, he gave a terse report of what they'd done, grabbing Paige when she went to help.

He yanked her hard against his body, his grip tightening when she rammed an elbow into his hard belly.

"Let them do their job," he growled against her ear. She turned to snarl at him but his gaze was oddly gentle. It was then she realized she was shaking from head to toe, barely keeping it together. She held her body rigidly and sucked in an unsteady breath, praying she wouldn't fall apart until she was alone.

Ty's heat finally seeped into her limbs. She didn't know how he did it, considering he was as wet as she was. She forced herself to move away. "I'm f-fine. You don't need to b-baby me. Harry…"

"Will be fine," he murmured, his big body a strong, warm wall at her back. "Thanks to you."

The last words were so soft she almost missed them and then wished she had when tears burned the backs of her eyes. She pressed a hand to her lips to keep them from wobbling.

"What if we're too late?" She bit down on her thumb as Frankie and Dale loaded Harry onto the stretcher. He suddenly looked old and frail and she needed to do something more than stand there and fall apart. "What if—?"

"You got to him, Paige," he interrupted firmly, detaining her when she went to follow the EMTs. "Why don't you go change into dry clothes? I'll drive you to the hospital."

"No," she said, shrugging off his hand. "I'm fine. I'll go in the ambulance. Besides, I know how much the thought of going to the hospital scares you," and hurried from the kitchen.

When he was finally alone, Ty shoved an exasperated hand through his hair and released his breath. "I am not scared," he muttered irritably. And when the silence mocked him, he cursed. Then, because it was more satisfying, he cursed her.

If he was scared, it wasn't of going to a hospital where he might never be able to fulfil his passion.

It was Paige.

She terrified him; with her huge eyes…and her damn open, engaging smile. A smile that he'd missed over the past few days—more than he wanted to admit. A smile that made *him* smile just thinking about it.

And the look in her eyes when she'd watched the

EMTs load Harry onto the stretcher had momentarily rendered him stupid and made him forget her fierce independence. She'd been more than clear the other night had been a one-off thing. At the time he'd thought it was what he wanted too, but the past couple of days he'd barely seen her and... He sighed. He'd missed her, *dammit*.

So he'd come to Port St. John's to be alone...big deal. Everyone deserved some alone time without being badgered and called a coward.

Little Miss Medic expected him to carry on as if everything was fine. But *nothing* was fine. Not his damn hand, not his uncertain future and certainly not the way he kept thinking about her when she wasn't around. Thinking about the way her breath hitched an instant before she surrendered...the breathy moans she made when he brushed his fingers over her soft skin and the look on her face when she came.

Cursing up a storm, Ty repacked the emergency kit.

She was just a woman, he reminded himself. A little more annoying and bossy than most, but still...just...a...woman.

So what the hell was his problem with Paige?

"Absolutely no problem at all," he snarled to

the empty house. "Besides, why the hell should I care if Miz Independence wants to pretend nothing happened? In fact, I'm relieved." A muscle twitched in his jaw. "No, I'm ecstatic," he muttered through clenched teeth. "Because now I can go home, have a nice long shower and move on without having to worry about bossy, annoying pain-in-the-ass distractions."

Realizing that he was starting to sound like a crazy person, he set his jaw and stomped over to the doors leading to the deck. He locked them with an impatient twist of his wrist and looked around for Harry's house keys because there was no question the old man would be admitted for observation and tests. And to ensure that happened, Ty reached for his phone to call his father. Henry Chapman had been Harry's doctor for thirty-five years and would want to know.

But Ty couldn't find his phone anywhere. After searching the entire house, he remembered that Paige had picked it up to call emergency. She'd most likely shoved it into her pocket without thinking.

Finally, Ty locked the house and stomped back home. When he caught himself *thinking* of it as home, he paused, oblivious to the wind blowing snow into his face and down his wet shirt.

What the—? Oh, no. No way. This freezing, storm-battered town was *not* home and the sooner he returned to his life in balmy Malibu the better.

He'd hit his favorite beach, he decided darkly, and cuddle up to some lithe, tanned beach bunnies who wanted nothing more than a good time.

Yeah. A good time sounded…good. No, it sounded great.

Muttering, he stormed through his front door and promptly fell over something lying just inside. Swearing, he picked himself off the floor and in the light of his torch saw Paige's shoulder bag, its contents spilled across the floor.

Dammit, the woman needed a damn keeper. She was a walking disaster. But he was not—*would not be*—anyone's keeper. Especially a woman who'd blown his mind with her soft mouth and sensual moans then turned around and pretended *he* was the annoying neighbor.

Shaking his head at all the stuff women carried in their handbags, Ty began stuffing everything back. When he came across her keys, wallet, cell-phone and lip gloss, he sighed and rose.

Looked like he wouldn't be moving on just yet.

At least not until he made sure she got home okay.

Despite the ugly road conditions, he made it to the hospital without incident and headed straight for ER. It was like a scene from a television medical drama and Ty wished he was a million miles away.

He sucked in air, conscious of his pounding pulse and the constriction in his chest. On a purely intellectual level he realized he was having a mild panic attack. His testosterone scoffed at the idea and he forced himself forward.

Casting a quick glance over the room, he decided that no one appeared in any immediate danger and went looking for Paige. He spotted her bent over a chart, bedraggled and wet. She muttered something and turned abruptly, uttering a little yelp of surprise when she ran into him. He shot out a hand to keep her from falling over a nearby crash cart.

"T-Ty? What are you doing here?"

She was pale and lines of stress pinched the area around her eyes. His gut clenched hard.

"Harry?"

She stared at him for a couple of beats. Her

throat worked as though she was having trouble getting the words out and then her eyes abruptly filled. *Aw, man.*

His chest squeezed and with a muttered curse he gently pulled her in, instantly struck by her terrifying fragility.

She was such a tough, feisty woman that her tears sliced at him with sharp claws.

"Dammit, Paige," he murmured into her damp, tousled hair. "I'm sorry. I'm so damn sorry. Harry is….he's special to you, isn't he?" He set his jaw, finding her tears more devastating because she was so determined not to fall apart.

In the course of his job he often had to give people bad news about their loved ones. It was never easy, but Paige…dammit, she slayed him. His throat tight with an emotion he couldn't name, Ty tightened his arms around and murmured soothing words into her hair. He was determined to be there for her, if only it—like their night—was this one time.

Finally she sucked in a deep breath and lifted her head. They were so close Ty could see his reflection in the tears clinging to her inky lashes. And felt himself fall. Hard. Right into her huge damp eyes. Right into the swirl of blue and green and gold.

And for the first time in his life he experienced the air being sucked from his lungs—heck, from the entire universe—leaving his mind in chaos and his heart and lungs aching like he'd been kicked in the chest.

Oblivious to his inner turmoil, Paige gave a ragged laugh and dropped her forehead against his chest. "He's… I think he's going to be okay," she murmured. "He came to in the ambulance. Dr. Chapman… I mean your…f-father…sent him for a bunch of tests but his vitals look promising." She drew in a shaky breath and stepped away to brush impatiently at the tears on her cheeks. "Anyway…" she grimaced and took the clipboard a nurse thrust at her as she hurried past "…we're swamped."

"I thought your shift was over," Ty began, but Paige was already moving away, her attention clearly on a mother and child nearby.

"Paige?"

She flung over her shoulder, "Look, I'll see you later. Maybe." She stopped abruptly and turned, her gaze searching. "Are you okay? Being here, I mean?"

"I'm fine," he growled with exasperation, ignoring the urge to get the hell out so he could feel fresh air on his face. Paige's gaze was searching and he sighed, holding his arms out at his side. "See. Fine."

Paige expelled an exasperated breath and said in a tone that suggested she was rolling her eyes, "Okay, you're fine," she muttered, and turned away, only to stop and swing around. "In that case, will you look in on Harry? See he's got everything he needs, I mean?"

Ty murmured that he would and was still standing there, embarrassed by his outburst, when his father appeared beside him.

"Tyler," Henry Chapman greeted him with a worried frown. Lines of tension bracketed his eyes and mouth as he took in Ty from head to toe. Upon seeing Ty unharmed his frown eased. "You're okay."

"I'm fine, Dad." He sighed and caught himself rolling *his* eyes because everyone thought he was a wuss. "Harry's skin was grey and clammy when we found him and we have no idea how long he'd been unconscious."

"He's a tough one," Henry mused. "But he admitted to being sick the last few days. It's probably just electrolytes, but we're running a full battery of tests. You made a good call there, son, giving him magnesium and honey."

"It was Paige's idea."

"Paige...?" Henry's expression cleared and he laughed. "Oh, you mean our ER pediatrician." He turned to look around and Ty's gaze followed to where she gave an abashed mountain of a guy a piece of her mind. "She's a little firecracker, isn't she? We were exceptionally lucky to get her. The kids love her."

"Dad, about that. Why don't you put her in Paeds instead of ER?"

Henry shook his head. "We don't have the funds for a children's ward, Tyler, and no specialist to run it. I try to send all the under-twelves to her but my request for a children's wing and a full-time pediatrician is under review. Besides, she's only here to pay back her student loans and we can't offer what those big city hospitals can. I'm hoping to change her mind but until then..." He looked around. "Look, I have to go. Dinner Sunday?"

Ty shocked himself by saying, "Will it be okay with Rhonda?" He'd met his father's new wife—a retired high school science teacher—but had avoided any family dinners because the truth was, somewhere down deep was that kid who wanted to punish his father for not playing a more active role in his life. But he was thirty-five years old, for God's sake, too old to be harboring grudges like an angry adolescent.

Henry sent him a sharp look. "Of course it's okay. It's your home too." He caught sight of someone trying to get his attention. "I'd better go." He started walking off but paused to say across his shoulder, "Oh, and that cute girl?" Amusement gleamed in eyes the exact shade of Ty's. "The one who beat you up?" Henry chuckled at Ty's expression. "Bring her too. You need a little fun in your life. God knows, life with your mother wasn't easy but not all women are like Renée, son." He inclined his head towards Paige. "And that little girl has the biggest heart of anyone I know. Just looking at her makes me smile."

Ty shoved a hand through his hair and sighed. Just looking at her made him smile too. It also made him think about things a son shouldn't be thinking in front of his father. "She's not a little girl, Dad," he reminded Henry mildly. "She's a specialist."

"And a damned good one too," Henry retorted.

"But look at her, son. Doesn't she just light up the room?"

Clearly Harry hadn't expected an answer because he immediately headed off, leaving Ty to watch Paige until she disappeared into an exam room. Irritated with himself, he shook off the odd pang of loneliness, because if his childhood had taught him anything, it was that he didn't like leaving things up to chance. He wanted to know his next course of action and he'd learned to ignore things he couldn't control.

Like relationships and feelings.

Because who the hell could control those?

And then there was Paige Carlyle. His father was right. She did light up a room; whether with her smile or her big eyes that sparkled with the same wonder and enthusiasm as the little kids she treated, she tended to draw people to her like a moth to a flame.

And Ty wasn't any different.

He'd come to Washington to be alone and make decisions about his future. Instead he'd spent most of it deliberately avoiding thinking about what he would do if he couldn't be a trauma surgeon and actively seeking out a woman who didn't want anything more from him than he had to offer.

And it was driving him nuts.

Yeah, shocking, he admitted wryly, especially as he'd never wanted anything more from women than brief mutually satisfying affairs. Paige didn't fit into any mold and she was independent to a fault. She'd also turned his ordered existence upside down, leaving him floundering in a sea of frustration and emotional turmoil.

He liked order, dammit, and he liked control; neither of which could be equated with Paige Carlyle, and brought back memories of his childhood he'd rather forget.

When a passing nurse sent him a curious look he realized he'd been standing there scowling like a crazy person. Sighing, Ty turned and headed for the exit, determined to regain control of his life.

He was almost at his car when he realized he hadn't asked for his phone and that he still had her keys, lip gloss and phone. Sighing, he retraced his steps and approached the nurses' station. He would hand over her keys and wallet and leave.

And that would be that.

On impulse he sent the frazzled nurse a friendly smile and, leaning forward, said, "Can you do me a favor?"

Her eyes widened and she went pink. "Um…
sure, what can I do for you?"

"Two things actually." He flashed a quick look
at her name tag. "Nurse Tucker, is it?"

"It's Nancy." The woman dimpled with pleasure and fluttered her eyelashes. "And if it gets
me another sexy smile, I'll have your babies too."

The other nurse at the station snorted and said,
"I'd like to know what your *husband* would say
to that, Nance."

"Oh, shoo, Shaz!" Nancy giggled. "A woman's
entitled to flirt a little." She winked at Ty. "So
what can I do for you, handsome?"

"It's for Paige Carlyle."

"You mean Dr. Cutie?"

His mouth curled at the moniker Paige couldn't
seem to shake. "Yep. Can you dig up some dry
scrubs for her? Oh, and when she's finished for
the night I want you to stall her."

Nancy and the other nurse shared a curious
look. "No problem with the scrubs, consider it
done. But…she's already put in a full shift and…"

"Long enough to call me," he explained. "She
came in the ambulance with Mr. Andersen and
needs a lift home."

Nancy looked unsure for a moment and Ty understood that they were protecting Paige from potential crazy stalkers. He dug his wallet out of his pocket and pulled out his ID.

"Henry Chapman will vouch for me," he said, showing her the ID.

"All right, Tyler Reese," Nancy said, her flirtatious smile back in full force. "And what number should I call?"

Ty rattled off his number before realizing that Paige still had his phone. "No wait, call Dr. Carlyle's cell number, she still has mine." He could see Nancy's curiosity bump up a couple of notches but she promised to call him when Paige was finished for the night.

Ty thanked her and left, ignoring the voice in his head demanding to know what the hell he thought he was doing.

He didn't have any answers. He only knew that his life was as out of control as his feelings for one sexy, pain-in-the-ass distraction.

CHAPTER TEN

IT WAS AFTER ten when Ty parked in front of the house and killed the engine. He'd stopped at an all-night burger joint despite Paige's insistence that she wasn't hungry.

"You didn't have to wait for me," she said for the tenth time in as many minutes. "Especially when you're afraid of hospitals."

Ty opened his door with a look of exasperation. "I'm not afraid of damn hospitals. And I didn't wait. I got Nancy to call me. End of story." He got out and shut the door.

Her eyes tracked him, big and capable and a little irritated, as he rounded the hood. *Okay.* She rolled her eyes.

Clearly *that* discussion was over.

Shivering in the freezing air that had invaded the interior, she looked around for her shoulder bag and was just about to freak out when she remembered that she hadn't had it with her in the ambulance.

It reminded her of Harry and her heart squeezed before she remembered that he was fine. She'd already checked on him and he was sleeping comfortably, which was a lot better than the alternative. She paused a moment to wonder what would have happened if Bertha hadn't started that afternoon. No one would have thought to check on him and—

The passenger door opened abruptly and she gave a startled squeak. "*Omigod*, will you stop doing that?" she gasped, glaring up into Ty's dark face. "And shut the door. It's freezing."

He studied her silently for a moment. "You planning on sleeping in the car?" he enquired mildly, easily holding the door open and snagging the bag of food that she'd been hugging to her chest.

"Well, not anymore. *Yeesh*," she grumbled, sliding out to stand shivering on the sidewalk in thin oversized scrubs and a huge jacket Ty had found in the back of his car. "I don't suppose you'll consider doing your breaking and entering thing again?" She hunched into the jacket for warmth. "I have no idea what I did with my purse or keys."

Ty nudged her away from the car and closed the door, locking it with a *beep-beep* of his remote. "I don't suppose," he said mildly, grabbing her hand

and practically frog-marching her up the path to his door. She tried to swerve towards her own door, but he simply yanked her after him.

"Dammit," she muttered, having to run to keep up with his long legs. "You'd think with everything that's happened you'd make an exception." When he just snorted, she batted her eyelashes at him and asked sweetly, "What if I asked pretty please and promised not to call the cops? I know they scare you as much as hospitals do."

He made a sound of annoyance and nudged her up the stairs. "Cops and hospitals do not scare me," he said with exaggerated patience.

"But—"

"You do," he interrupted irritably. "You scare me."

That brought her up short. She gaped at him. "Me? I scare you?" She didn't know whether to be pleased or insulted.

Light spilled from overhead, giving the illusion of enclosing them in a cocoon of warmth. Despite being from California, the icy cold didn't appear to affect him. She didn't know why that surprised her as he was the kind of man that radiated heat and sexuality at a hundred paces. *Darn sexy alphas.*

Half his face was in darkness, the other half all

planes and angles that stole her breath. No one should look that good, she thought with dismay, huffing with annoyance when she caught a whiff of his delicious man scent. Who the heck smelled that good after a full hectic day and half the night? She probably smelled like disinfectant and other not-so-pleasant ER smells.

"Yes," he muttered, nudging her inside. "You scare the hell out of me."

His touch, after the stress of the day, had heat and excitement spinning through her so abruptly that she whirled around. "Well, then, maybe I should just go. Clearly you want to be alone— *Hey.*" Her hand jerked up in the universal "stop" gesture when he kept coming.

She didn't know what she was saying stop to but when her palm came into contact with a warm hard chest, alarm signals ran up her arm and into her brain. Signals that urged her to move the hell away.

Her brain might have been on board but her hand tingled with the urge to explore that wide expanse of muscle and sinew. Heat arrowed right up her arm into her chest and her nipples instantly tightened into painful little buds. *Yikes.* It felt like someone had touched a live wire to her skin, sending little pricks of current skating across her flesh.

Maybe she was just coming down with a chill, she thought. She'd been drenched at least four times today and—she mentally rolled her eyes—maybe her body hadn't received the message that she was over him.

She slowly lifted her gaze from where her fingers were stroking him, moving to the hollow of his throat where she really, *really* wanted to put her mouth; up past the hard square jaw that hadn't seen a razor since that morning to his finely sculpted mouth. She waited for him to say something...*anything*...so she could watch his mouth move, finally lifting her gaze when it didn't.

Unmistakable tension radiated from his big brawny body and Paige got caught in his sexy blue eyes.

Wait...*what?* Weren't they supposed to be done with this?

"Ty—" she began, snatching her hand away as though she'd been burned. She thrust it behind her and backed away, swallowing hard because she didn't want him thinking she couldn't keep her hands off him.

When her voice finally emerged it was breathless. "Maybe I should check on Harry, he—"

"You already checked. Five times," Ty interrupted in a deep voice that sent a delicious thrill through her. "He's going to be fine, Paige." He moved towards her, a large hungry cat on the prowl, a dangerous predator with Paige in his sights.

Oh, boy.

"He just needs a couple days on fluids and a change of meds." With his eyes on hers he kicked the door shut behind him, ratcheting Paige's pulse up a couple of hundred notches. "Before you know it he'll be back home, where you can keep an eye on him."

She nodded and nervously licked her lips, wondering what the heck she was thinking by entering his lair...uh, house. It was so much easier taking charge in her own space.

As though he knew what she was thinking, Ty took a couple of steps towards her, his mouth curving when her eyes widened and she sucked in a startled little breath.

Dammit, girl. Stop reacting like he's about to eat you instead of burgers. Narrowing her eyes, she stiffened her spine and stubbornly held her ground, even when he kept coming, only to stop a bare inch away.

Instantly his heat surrounded her, and she had to tip her head back because everyone knew that you had to face a predator to show you weren't afraid.

And she wasn't afraid...not exactly. She sighed. Okay, she was terrified. Terrified of the feelings turning her jittery and terrified of the hold he had on her, hijacking her dreams and stealing her peace of mind.

Finally, he broke the ratcheting tension by planting a hand against the wall behind her and leaning closer. Paige reacted like he'd shoved her, backing up to escape the heated web of need and want he so easily wove around her.

"What are you doing?" she squeaked breathlessly.

Without replying, he moved closer, then closer still, only pausing when his mouth was a whisper away from her ear. "Do you know what I want?" he breathed, his voice rough and deep and scraping along every exposed nerve ending.

Terrified of what it meant, she locked her knees and shook her head. "B-burgers?"

He stilled as though she'd surprised him and after a couple of beats he chuckled, the gravelly low sound sending hot and cold shivers dancing through her. "No." His lips brushed her throat. "Not burgers."

Paige's hands came up, and though she really intended to push him away, they curled tightly into his sweatshirt.

"Ty..." she began, torn between wanting desperately for him to kiss her and an overwhelming need to protect her heart. She instinctively knew that if he kissed her again, it wouldn't end there. And then she wouldn't be able to pretend that this was just a casual fling that she was totally over.

Her head thunked back against the wall in an attempt to knock some sense into it but her body had a mind of its own. Her hands did too, releasing their grip on his sweatshirt to smooth over hard abs and warm skin beneath his shirt.

He gave a laughing groan that drew Paige's attention to his mouth and—oh, God—she suddenly needed it more than she needed her next breath. In fact, she would probably die without it.

Like in the next two seconds.

"Ty," she breathed again, and even to her own ears it sounded like a plea. It momentarily cleared her head enough for her to say, "I thought you didn't want—"

"Oh, I want," he interrupted hoarsely. "I want…
another kiss…another night…" He shifted closer
and his breathing became as ragged as hers. "I'm
hoping…this'll finally do it."

Heat pooled low in her belly and her bones
began to melt, along with her resistance. "Do…
what?"

He closed the half-inch to take a nip out of her
mouth. "Get you out of my system," he growled,
slanting his mouth over hers and tracing her lips
with a line of fire. "Hopefully…for good, this
time." And then he sucked her bottom lip into
his mouth and brushed aside his jacket to cup her
breast through the thin scrubs.

She gave a ragged moan and arched into his
touch.

"Dammit," he breathed. "This wasn't supposed
to feel so good."

"So…good." And because he felt so good, Paige
smoothed her hands up his wide back, marveling
at the solid strength beneath her fingers and the
way his muscles shifted and bunched.

She couldn't remember ever wanting anyone
this badly.

She made a hungry sound in the back of her
throat, helpless against the need pounding through

her, wanting…needing more, especially when she canted her hips and found him big and hard and fully aroused.

She slid her hands around and down his chest and abs, curling her fingers into his jeans waistband. Mostly to hang onto and then, when his belly muscles clenched, to torture.

"Paige…*wait.*" His breath whooshed out and he grabbed her hands, lifting them away and pinning them to the wall above her head. "Be sure," he warned. "Because if you're not…dammit, say something before…before I lose what little control I'm hanging onto…and take you right here against the wall."

Suddenly Paige wanted to take that control. She wanted wild and fast because it had been that kind of day. Oh, and up against the wall sounded good.

Now even better.

With her hands still locked in his, she lifted her mouth and murmured, "Maybe just one more time—"

Before she could complete the sentence, Ty swooped down and caught her mouth in a hard, hungry kiss—a kiss that instantly turned lethal and had her body responding as though he hadn't satisfied her every sensual fantasy a few nights earlier.

He fed her hot open-mouthed kisses, his hands releasing her to sneak beneath her scrubs and rasp against naked flesh. The sensations rolling through her had her pressing closer, moaning in triumph and anticipation when he swelled and hardened against her belly.

Her breath caught and her core went hot and wet. Just as her knees gave way, Ty uttered something hot and explicit beneath his breath and swept her into his arms.

She squeaked at the abrupt change in elevation, clutching at his shoulders as he headed for the stairs. "Your sh-shoulder," she gasped.

His answer was a low huffing laugh as he took the stairs like he was in a hurry. And, *oh, boy*, Paige could certainly relate. She was in a hurry too. "What—what about…the wall?"

She'd have been okay with the wall.

Ty turned right when he reached the landing. "I have another wall in mind," he said, kicking open the bathroom door. He let her go, allowing her body to slide down the length of his.

And when her eyes rolled back in her head, he

gave her bottom a sharp slap and ordered, "Strip," reaching into the shower to turn on the water.

The position allowed Paige to admire the wide V of his shoulders that tapered to narrow hips and long, muscular legs. Oh, yeah, she thought, drooling. And those tight buns she dreamed about sinking her teeth into—

Ty turned and caught her hungrily eyeing his backside. He uttered the low masculine sound that never failed to send tingles skittering through her and he reached out to wrap his hand in the front of her scrubs top. With his eyes on hers, he slowly pulled her closer and when all that separated them was his hand, he growled, "Were you ogling my backside?"

Paige snickered and backed away, uttering a squeak of surprise as her top went flying over her head.

"Hey… *Oomph,*" she muttered against the sudden invasion of his mouth. He kissed her as he did everything else, with single-minded purpose; plundering the depths of her mouth as he pillaged her senses.

With each article of clothing that vanished he pressed hot, open-mouthed kisses against her skin, stealing her breath and making her moan for more. Undressing became a sensual feast of hands and mouths and hungry sounds. By the time they were naked, steam filled the bathroom.

When Ty paused to wrap his cast in a waterproof casing, Paige's hands examined his wide chest and her tongue flicked at his tight male nipples. She hummed her appreciation against his smooth warm skin and scored her nails down his spine to his tight buns, loving the rough laugh and warning growl emerging from deep in his chest.

He caught her hands and with his hot blue gaze on hers drew her into the shower. Breathless with excitement and anticipation, Paige half expected—hoped—he'd shove her up against the wall and have his merry way with her. But his gaze abruptly gentled as it probed hers as though he was searching for something.

"Ty...?"

"No more talking." Then he dipped his head and dropped a kiss on her mouth before firmly turning her away from him.

Confused, she craned her head around to see him reaching for the shampoo and squirting a dollop into his hand. She frowned. "I thought—" she began, only to have him interrupting once more.

"No talking," he growled, smoothing shampoo

over her head. "Close your eyes...and just feel." Then he gently washed her hair, slowly massaging her scalp until she sagged against him in a boneless, speechless mass.

"You warm yet?"

Paige could have told him that she was melting but her voice emerged on a low groan of pleasure and she couldn't even drum up the teeniest bit of offense when he laughed.

Once he'd rinsed her hair, he reached for the soap and proceeded to wash her with the same gentle strokes, taking extra care with her breasts, her belly...before moving to legs. And when her body tingled and her heart raced because surely now he would take her against the wall, he turned off the water and reached for a huge fluffy towel.

With his hot cobalt blue eyes locked on hers, Ty wrapped her up and carried her into the master bedroom. He paused beside the bed to drop a light kiss on her mouth and just when she began losing any sense of the world around them he broke the slight suction and tossed her unceremoniously into the middle of the bed.

She instantly bounced up with a laughing protest on her lips, only to be pushed flat when he followed her down.

His hungry mouth silenced her protest.

Surprised by the sudden change in his mood, she shoved at him and rolled them over until she was straddling his hips. "What was that?" she demanded breathlessly.

His answer was to chuckle and grab her hips. He pulled her snug against his erection, making them both groan. He took advantage of her distraction to cover her breasts with his big hands. Instantly she stilled, the sensations so lusciously decadent that her spine flexed and her head fell back in pleasure.

"This is me," he murmured, rearing up to brush his lips against the pulse pounding in her throat. "This is me taking control and getting you out of my system."

Paige clenched her thighs and sucked in a sharp breath at the feel of him, long and thick and hard between her legs. "How is it I'm the one on top, then?"

"This way," he rasped, dipping his head to catch one pebbled nipple between his teeth, "my hands are free." He spent a couple of seconds torturing her nipples before wrapping both arms around her and holding her close as he drew her flesh into his mouth.

She tried to say something but her mind slid away and there was nothing but Ty's mouth and hands sending her tumbling into heat and pleasure.

And when a dangerous thought slid into her mind—that she was playing with fire and this was as far from a fling as she could get—she pushed it aside because after tonight she'd be over him for good.

Accustomed to sleeping alone, Ty awakened sometime before dawn baffled by the warm soft presence beside him. He turned his head and in the dim light coming from the bathroom saw Paige still sprawled face down a couple of inches away. Her face was half-hidden by a silky curtain of inky hair.

Memories of how she'd got there flooded back and he couldn't have stopped himself from reaching out to smooth back that swing of hair any more than he could resist tracing a hand down the length of her spine to her soft, curvy bottom.

She gave a soft sigh and before he knew what he was doing, Ty had pulled her closer. With her back pressed to his front, he spent a minute enjoying the way her sleep-warmed curves fitted against him—as if she'd been fashioned with him in mind.

Murmuring sleepily, she snuggled closer and he slid one leg between hers, bending his knee as he reached around to palm one plump breast. Realizing that the position would prevent her from slipping away without him knowing, Ty smiled.

Let's see her sneak away from him now.

She stirred and murmured a sleepy, "Ty?"

"Yeah," he growled, pressing his lips to the back of her neck. "Expecting someone else?"

She yawned and stretched, arching against him in one long sinuous move. His body instantly responded until she said, "I dunno… Danny maybe, or…um… Nate?"

He sank his teeth into her shoulder, smiling against her skin when she made a sound between a snorting laugh and a yelp.

He couldn't remember ever laughing in bed with a woman before and when she asked sleepily if he wanted her to go, he tightened his hold on her and shocked himself by murmuring, "No, stay."

He lay awake for a long time listening to her breathe, wondering—not for the first time—what the hell he thought he was doing. He'd never wanted a woman to stay or wrapped her close to keep her from leaving. And he'd certainly never lain awake wanting more from her than she was willing to give.

Because, let's face it, he wasn't good with more. His life was in California and he'd never—*never*, he reminded himself sternly—considered changing it for a woman.

Still didn't.

Look at what had happened to his parents. They'd met at Stanford and the next thing they'd been married and living in Port St. John's. Henry had had big dreams of building the largest hospital on the Olympic Peninsula, a hospital that would serve the county, the town and the coastguard, as well as the entire length of the Juan de Fuca Strait.

His mother had hated it and when Ty had been two she'd packed him up and returned to California. And though he'd seen his father on the odd visit, he'd had to wait six years to spend summers in Washington. By that time they hadn't even known each other.

He'd once asked Henry why he'd never sued for custody or objected to Ty's change of name, and his father had replied that a child needed his mother.

Yeah, but Ty had needed his father too…away

from the stifling expectations of a woman who'd demanded perfection from her son and then frozen him out when he'd disappointed her.

It was no wonder he preferred to remain unattached. His childhood had been an emotional minefield and he'd buried his emotions until... *dammit*, until Paige.

But that didn't mean he was falling for her, he assured himself. It just meant he was bored and needed a distraction. And who better to distract him than his sassy neighbor?

Sometime later he felt movement and was instantly alert. "What's wrong?" he rasped, rolling over to see Paige carefully slipping off the bed. She jolted when he spoke but didn't turn around.

"I...uh...nothing, I just need the...um...bathroom."

Scrubbing a hand over his face, he watched as she snagged one of his T-shirts and pulled it over her head. He wanted to object to her covering all those sweet curves but she was already pulling away from him. And despite what he'd said last night, he wasn't ready to let her go.

Not yet.

Sitting up, he studied her through narrowed lids. "You were sneaking out, weren't you?"

"What? No," she said quickly, and to Ty's mind guiltily. Her eyes slid away. "Of course not. What makes you think that?"

He searched her face for a hint of what she was thinking but for once her expression was unreadable.

"It might have something to do with the way you're avoiding looking at me," he drawled.

She fidgeted nervously, tugging at the hem of his T-shirt, although Ty could have told her not to bother. He'd already seen every inch of her and liked what he'd seen…and touched…and tasted.

His body stirred and his mouth began to water. He also liked seeing her all flustered, especially when she thrust a hand through her hair and began to mutter to herself. She clearly didn't know what to do with her hands because she finally huffed out a breath and stuck them into her armpits.

"It's just… I'm not good…with *this*," she said defensively, edging towards the door and sending him quick nervous looks as though she expected him to pounce and needed a head start.

Beginning to enjoy himself, Ty propped a hand behind his head. "What's 'this' exactly?"

She thrust out her bottom lip and blew out an

exasperated breath and although he couldn't see her eyes, he suspected that she was rolling them.

"This…" She gestured wildly, including his entire room. "This…um, after stuff."

"You mean after hot sex?"

A wild flush rose into her cheeks and Ty took pity on her, tossing back the sheet and rising. He paused to stretch and heard a strangled sound catch in Paige's throat. Her eyes widened at the sight of his morning erection and when he said, "Why don't we—?" she whirled and a second later the bathroom door slammed.

Grinning, Ty pulled on a pair of jeans and on his way past the bathroom he called out, "I was about to say let's go out for breakfast. But if you're up for shower sex, I'm game."

Her reply was incomprehensible and in the form of a muffled squeak, making Ty laugh. "Okay, but if you're not out in five minutes, I'm coming in."

CHAPTER ELEVEN

IT WASN'T OFTEN that Paige and Frankie had a day off together but when they did, they liked doing something they wouldn't normally. Last time they'd gone hiking—not Paige's favorite pastime, although the scenery had made up for the unpleasant physical exertion.

It had been Paige's turn to choose and she was eager to explore all the little towns along the coast. Frankie, naturally athletic, had smirked at Paige's choice of outing but with the promise of lunch at the charming Three Orcas Restaurant, overlooking a rocky bay, she'd reluctantly agreed on condition that Paige paid.

They'd managed an early start and headed for the scenic route to an artists' colony nestled in a bay a couple of hours up the coast.

Paige had jumped at the chance to get out of Port St. John's, needing to clear her head of all the intoxicating male pheromones making her crazy.

Although she was enjoying having Ty around, she kept waiting for the other shoe to drop.

He'd been in Washington for nearly six weeks and she knew without being told that he would soon be returning to LA. She'd casually mentioned his check-up a few times but whenever she did he either shut down completely or he'd put his hands and mouth on her and then she not only forgot what they were discussing, she forgot her own name.

She understood that he was worried about how his hand would impact his future but she couldn't help being hurt that he refused to discuss his concerns with her.

But that was okay, she told herself, they were just neighbors. Granted, they were neighbors with benefits, but Ty was hot, she was willing, and they enjoyed each other's company. End. Of. Story.

Besides, ever since the storm they'd fallen into a kind of unspoken routine where Paige would go to work and Ty would spend time with his father, Nate or Harry. When she got home, he'd badger her about her eating habits, and more often than not make her dinner.

Suddenly she was spending more and more nights in his bed and she was afraid that when he left she wouldn't be able to sleep alone. Her mom had been gone more than fifteen years and it was strange having someone around to nag her about eating properly and getting enough rest. Paige couldn't remember anyone else ever making the effort. If she didn't know any better she could almost convince herself that he cared.

But that was dangerous thinking and although she tried not to, she began looking forward to eating home-cooked meals she didn't have to prepare.

Okay, so she enjoyed his company and whatever came after dinner—and sometimes before—was good too. *Big deal.* What woman wouldn't get excited fantasizing about coming home after a long day in ER to a hot sexy guy, a home-cooked meal and great sex?

Well, Paige was no dummy. She was going to enjoy it while it lasted, without getting her feelings hurt or her heart involved. She'd learned early that people didn't stick and when they bailed you got your heart stomped on. But that wasn't going to happen because her heart wasn't involved with Ty.

Nope, it was locked away safe and sound.

But her body…well, that was something else

entirely. Her body craved him with an intensity that would have scared her if she let herself think about it.

So she didn't.

She shoved it to the back of her mind and never made the mistake of waking up with him again, having discovered the emotional intimacy of mornings-after made her feel exposed.

And feeling exposed—especially with a man like Ty—would be fatal. Better to slip away and pretend they were just friendly neighbors. Besides, he'd never mentioned her early-morning Houdini acts so he was clearly happy with the way things were.

Well, good. Fine. She was happy too.

Especially as she was about to spend a glorious day with her best friend.

Once on the highway, Paige opened her window, cranked up the volume of the radio and sang along to every song—even when she didn't know the words. After snorting at her creative lyrics, Frankie joined in and pretty soon they were laughing like loons.

It was exactly what Paige needed; a fun day away from all the confusing emotions she didn't know what to do with. Besides, she needed a healthy dose of reality and could always count on Frankie's perceptive smartass-ness to make her laugh.

They stopped for morning tea at a quaint little seaside café so Paige could stuff her face with waffles smothered in fresh berries and cream.

By midmorning they'd pulled into Battle Bay and set out to explore the quaint little galleries filled with hundreds of paintings depicting life on the Olympic Peninsula.

They headed over to watch craftsmen and -women work. It was fascinating and educational, especially the candle sculpting, but Frankie had been more interested in the artist creating huge metal sea creatures. That the guy had been hot and shirtless hadn't escaped their attention and Frankie had spent an inordinate amount of time photographing...well, his artwork too.

By the time they were headed back to Port St. John's, Paige was feeling mellow for the first time in weeks. Life on an emotional roller-coaster was exhausting and she was looking forward to her life getting back to normal.

Liar.

Ignoring the disgusted voice in her head, she thought instead about the gifts she'd bought for

Ty and Harry. She'd chosen an amazingly realistic carving of a coastguard cutter for Harry and a fierce-looking eagle for Ty.

She couldn't wait to see his reaction.

"You know," Frankie said lazily when they were about fifteen minutes from home, "this was actually a fun day. We should do it again. Maybe sleep over somewhere and make a weekend of it."

Paige hummed her agreement. "I knew you'd like it."

"What I liked," Frankie drawled, "was seeing that guy Matt Rolfe with his shirt off." She hummed. "That was the highlight of the day."

Paige giggled. "I thought it was the crab salad and Manhattan iced tea."

Frankie waggled her brows.

"So I guess all those photos you were taking weren't of his artwork?" Paige asked.

When Frankie gave a snorted "Puh-*leeze*", she momentarily took her gaze off the road.

"Shame on you. Is that why you asked him if he ever posed in the nude?"

Her friend rolled her eyes and fanned her face. "Did you see that guy? *He* was the work of art. Boy, I sure learned a whole lot about art appreciation today."

"He was okay, I guess," Paige mused, thinking about another man she wouldn't mind painting in the nude—if she had any talent, that was. But her stick figures could hardly be termed as talent.

She was enjoying the image of painting a naked Ty with chocolate paint—stuff she could lick off—and almost missed Frankie's horrified sideways look.

"Okay? Are you nuts?" Her friend whipped off her sunglasses to gape at Paige. "With all those gleaming muscles and a great butt showcased in faded denim, the man was the embodiment of the statue of David. Holy cow, I nearly swooned at his feet."

"Mmm," Paige said, unimpressed. "Have you looked at David? I mean, *really* looked?"

"Well, not as much as I looked at Matt Rolfe," she confessed. "But what are you getting at?"

"I did a study on David in art class and, well... he's a little small."

"What are you talking about? That statue is huge."

Paige snickered. "Not where it, um...counts it isn't."

Grinning widely, Frankie said in an echo of Paige's previous statement, "Shame on you, Paige

Carlyle, but believe me when I say Matt Rolfe filled out his jeans just fine. And just because you're getting some, it doesn't mean the rest of us aren't looking." She glanced at Paige. "Or aren't jealous as hell. Especially with that goofy smile you wear most of the time."

"What?" Paige blinked innocently and made a show of looking at her reflection in the rearview mirror. "What goofy smile?" She hadn't said anything about how she'd been spending her nights, mostly because she'd barely seen Frankie since the night of the storm. Oh, yes, and maybe because she didn't know what the heck to say except... *wow* and...*holy cow.*

"Don't try that with me, Dr. Cutie. With both you and Ty looking all relaxed and mellow, it's obvious what's been going on."

"Nothing's been going on," Paige insisted, her mellow mood vanishing. Nothing *was* happening. Well, except for a lot of amazing orgasms...but nobody needed to know about those. "And when did you see Ty?"

"The other evening when you were on duty. Didn't he tell you?"

"No, um... I guess it didn't come up."

"Well I was at the Seafarers when he and Nate

came in and I overheard them discussing his accident."

"His accident?" Paige said, trying to sound casual because Ty certainly hadn't shared much of anything personal with her, especially his accident.

"Yeah, well, after what I heard, I did an internet search on it and apparently some drunk guy thought Ty was someone else and tried to run him over. Fortunately the bumper only clipped him or it would have been a lot worse than a few bruises and a couple of broken bones." She shook her head. "A real pity as he's supposed to be one of the top trauma surgeons at St Augustine's."

Frankie frowned and turned to Paige. "And why didn't you tell me he's leaving next week?"

Paige's mind went blank. "I...um— What?"

Frankie's gaze sharpened and she cursed softly. "You didn't know. Damn, Paige. I'm sorry."

Paige rallied quickly and casually hitched her shoulder. "Don't be," she said, sending her friend a dazzling smile that probably fell way short of its intended brilliance. "Of course I knew he was leaving...just not next... You know it doesn't matter because it's not like we're a thing...or anything," she finished lamely.

Frankie sounded skeptical. "So hot regular sex isn't a thing?"

"Of course not," Paige spluttered out on a strangled laugh. "We barely know each other and—"

"And you're in love with him."

"What? *No*," she squeaked, wrenching the wheel and nearly driving into oncoming traffic. After righting the car, she turned to gape at Frankie like she'd announced something horrifying. Because she had...kind of. Horrifying and *so-o-o* not true. "Of course I'm not in love with Ty." That would be ridiculous and really, really stupid.

"Stupid I give you," Frankie retorted, and it took a couple of seconds for Paige to realize she'd spoken out loud. "But what's so ridiculous about it? Is it because he might never do surgery again? Because if it is—"

"What?" Paige demanded indignantly. "Are you crazy? Of course that's not the reason. He's leaving, so whether or not I'm in love with him— and I'm *not*," she insisted when Frankie rolled her eyes, "is beside the point. He's leaving." Oh, boy, it was finally happening. "Maybe now I can get some sleep." Her heart squeezed and she got a very bad feeling in her stomach. Hopefully it was just the crab she'd had for lunch because the alternative was— *No. Nope. Not happening.* "End of story," she said firmly, although she wasn't sure who she was talking to.

"Sleeping's overrated," Frankie dismissed with a flick of her hand. "You can sleep when you're—" She sat up abruptly and swore. "What the hell is that driver—? Hey, watch out!"

Her warning came too late for Paige to swerve out of the way and was drowned out by the sound of crunching metal and shattering glass. The last thing she heard was Frankie's curse.

Ty raced through the automatic doors at the JDF Medical Center and headed straight for ER. The nurse at the sign-in desk looked up as he ran past.

"Hey!" She bolted around the counter and grabbed his sleeve. "You can't go through there. Stop!"

Ty whirled on her, breathing fast. He probably looked like a wild man but he didn't care. Only that he—

"Paige Carlyle," he snarled. "Which room?"

The woman's brow wrinkled. "I don't know… Dr. Michaels, I think…she—"

"I'll find her," he growled through clenched teeth, shaking off her hand and heading for the swing doors separating the waiting area from the exam rooms. The door closed on her spluttered, "We're in Code Yellow."

The place was in chaos. Nurses, orderlies and paramedics rushed about and he could hear a furious male voice snap, "Find her, before I have all your asses in a sling."

It was the first time he'd been in the belly of ER since his accident but the fact that his chest was squeezing the life out of him had nothing to do with apprehension about his future, cardiac arrest or even that he was afraid he'd never work in another ER again.

All he could think about was the call he'd received fifteen minutes ago from Nate. Sitting on Harry's deck, playing chess, he'd been enjoying the sun and the old man's stories about his glory days as a coastguard. One minute he'd been chuckling and plotting his move, the next...

"There's been an accident," Nate had said brusquely without his customary greeting, and his next words had sent Ty's world into a tailspin. Nate barely got out, "Paige is..." and Ty had already vaulted off Harry's deck.

"That was Nate," he'd called out, dashing the few yards along the marina walkway and taking the stairs to his deck at a dead run. "There's been an accident." He'd said nothing about Paige in case Harry worried, but the drive to the hospital had been the longest fifteen minutes of his life; even longer than waiting for the orthopedic surgeon to pronounce his diagnosis after his surgery. Even longer than waiting in a jail cell at eighteen for his mother to arrive.

And now, with the current chaos, the worst possible scenarios flashed through his head. At the center was Paige, battered, bruised and the cause of all the panic.

He grabbed the first person he came across, the nurse from the night of the storm. "Nancy—"

"Can't talk now, handsome," she hurriedly called out. "We've misplaced a...something."

He was about to ask her what the hell they'd misplaced when she raced off, leaving Ty to search every ER room himself.

He found her in the last room.

Not on the gurney, hooked up to IVs or machines, as he'd expected, but comforting the middle-aged woman on the bed. "Oh, my gosh, I'm so sorry," the woman sobbed. "I took that bend too fast and when I pumped the brakes there was...

nothing. Not a thing." She paused to wipe her eyes. "I didn't see you, I really didn't."

Ty froze in the doorway, his eyes racing over Paige, his heart pounding so hard he was surprised to see his chest intact. He opened his mouth but when nothing emerged he closed it with a snap.

The sight of her clearly in one piece caused something like a brain explosion and it took a few moments before he found his voice. "What the hell are you doing?" he rasped furiously.

Paige jolted like she'd been shot and flashed a startled look over her shoulder. The sight of a bruise blooming along her cheekbone had his anger rising in tandem with relief. Stalking closer, he whipped her around.

"Dammit, Paige," he growled, freezing when she winced and he got a good look at her face. Her eye was swollen, she had a vivid bruise along one side of her face, and a laceration that had yet to be attended to. Blood trickled from the wound and one side of her shirt was covered with blood.

"What the hell?" he rasped. "I thought…" He didn't complete his sentence, mostly because his throat closed; instead, he yanked her into his arms and crushed her close, his relief at seeing her, a little battered but very much alive, so immense that for a moment his knees buckled.

He locked them and tightened his grip on her, needing the feel of her in his arms probably more than she did. She cried out and he immediately let her go. "Damn, I'm sorry," he murmured, carefully stepping back so he could look her over. "Why haven't you been seen and why are you attending to someone else?"

"A patient has gone missing," she explained. "Everyone's busy and I'm not a priority."

"You damn well are," he snapped out, and took her arm before turning to the wide-eyed woman on the bed. "Ma'am, are you okay?"

The woman blinked. "I, um…sure. My son is on his way and your…your wife was kind enough to sit with me while I wait for a scan. But I'm fine. You go ahead."

"Ty—" Paige began, only to stop with a huff when he sent her a look that usually had ER personnel scattering.

He turned to the woman. "Excuse us while I attend to my…*wife*."

He pulled Paige into the opposite room and led her to the bed. "On," he said tersely, and when she made an annoyed sound in the back of her throat he sighed and growled, "Please."

"Ty, I'm fine," she began, gingerly getting onto the bed. "You didn't need to come."

"I came," he gritted out, "because I thought—probably stupidly—that you might need me." He didn't say that the thought of her being seriously injured had scared the living spit out of him. He didn't tell her that his mind had gone utterly blank and that at one point he'd thought he was having a coronary.

Getting madder, he slammed open drawers and cabinets, looking for what he'd need, before turning to find her sitting on the bed, watching him with serious eyes, her soft mouth pressed into a firm line. As though he'd done something reprehensible.

"You didn't have to come," she repeated dully. "As you can see, I'm fine."

"I'll be the judge of that," he growled, wanting more than anything to wrap her close and never let go. Or maybe wrap his fingers around her neck for scaring him.

The latter impulse was less frightening than the former and allowed him to focus. With his jaw clenched, he gently cleaned Paige's head wound, relieved to find it was just a little over an inch long and wouldn't even need stitches.

"What happened?" he asked when he'd calmed down enough to talk without snarling.

"Mrs. Eberhart said her brakes failed."

"I heard that part. What happened, Paige?"

She winced when he touched a particularly tender spot and huffed out a breathy growl like she was irritated. She didn't know the meaning of irritated, he thought furiously.

"I don't know," she said. "We were just up the coast and Frankie and I were talking about—well, never mind that." She flashed him an unreadable glance before continuing. "We were approaching a particularly steep bend and the next thing this red car came out of nowhere. It swerved into our lane and— Damn, that stings." She sucked in a sharp breath when he applied antiseptic but after a couple of beats she continued, her voice tight. "Anyway, I didn't swerve in time. She hit the driver's side and we…um…we spun into a section of rock face."

She was silent while he taped the wound closed. "You didn't have to do this, you know. Frankie would have—"

"Shut up," he interrupted quietly, and picked up the ophthalmoscope. "How bad is the headache?"

"I'm f—all right," she said huffily when he shone the light into her eyes and pain lanced through her skull. "I have a headache. Big deal. It happens when you rap your head against something." She pushed his hand away. "Just give me a damn aspirin and I'll be good to go." She made to slide off the bed but Ty put his hand on her chest to keep her there and she made an odd sound and froze.

"What? What's wrong?" he demanded, his eyes sweeping over her for signs of trauma he hadn't yet picked up. In the process he caught sight of her bruised wrist. "Dammit, why the hell didn't you say something?"

"Ty." She caught his hand and wrapped her fingers around his wrist. "It's just a bruise, I promise."

He flexed his jaw. "What else, Paige? A bruised wrist doesn't make you go white with pain."

For long moments she just looked at him as though she expected him to give up. But Ty wasn't anybody's fool. During his ER rotation he'd treated everything from crush injuries to impalements and knew when someone wasn't being straight with him.

Finally, Paige sighed and slowly lifted her T-shirt and it was Ty's turn to suck in air. He carefully helped her lift her shirt the rest of the way and cursed when he saw the line of bruising across her chest and abdomen from the car's seat belt. "Lie flat for me," he murmured, and when Paige snorted, he chuckled. "This is purely professional, believe me."

He gently probed her ribs, watching her face for a reaction she wouldn't be able to hide from him, and then listened to her chest for internal trauma. Finally he grunted in satisfaction and pulled her shirt down. He helped her sit up.

"Let's wrap that wrist, shall we?"

"Your hand—"

"Is just fine," he interrupted briskly. "A lot better than yours."

He found a crepe bandage and carefully strapped her wrist. He struggled a bit with the clips until she reached out with her good hand to help. Finally there was nothing more to do but Ty didn't move away. Instead, he lifted her chin and with his gaze locked on hers he kissed her carefully on the mouth.

His lips clung to hers, needing the connection more than he'd thought possible. After a long moment of unresponsiveness she uttered a soft sound and her…lips…melted.

Thank God. He'd been beginning to think that she was deliberately distancing herself from him. He changed the angle of the kiss and—

The door slammed open. "Paige, we have a blue thirt— Oh… Oh, I'm sorry," the nurse said when she took in the scene. She was about to back out of the room when Paige shoved Ty aside with her good hand and eased off the bed.

She looked a little dazed. "What about a b-blue thirteen?" she stuttered, her cheeks blooming with the color she'd been missing a short while ago. It took a moment for the RN's words to register and although not all hospitals used a code blue thirteen, he knew it meant an infant in distress.

"Paige, I'm s-sorry. I wouldn't ask you to do this…not after all you've b-been through." The woman's eyes filled. "Everyone else is busy and I don't know what to do."

"It's okay, Beth," Paige said, turning to snag a lab coat and stethoscope as she hurried from the room. "I'm fine, really. Lead the way."

Concerned, Ty followed. "Paige, don't tell me

you're going to treat a patient while you have a possible concussion."

She looked over her shoulder as the nurse handed her a clipboard. "I have a hard head. I'll get over it," she said, and Ty got an odd feeling she wasn't talking about her head. She turned away to scan the hastily scribbled notes before pausing to flash him a look that was curiously closed and devoid of her usual spark. "I know how hard this was for you. But I just want to thank you. For everything."

And the next instant she was gone, leaving Ty to stare at the corner around which she'd disappeared and wonder what the hell had just happened. It had seemed like she was saying goodbye. Like she would never see him again. Like... His chest squeezed.

"What the hell just happened?" he demanded, and though he'd spoken out loud, he certainly didn't expect anyone to reply from directly behind him.

"What happened where?"

He knew it was Frankie even before he turned but the sight of her had him taking a step back. "Jeez, woman, I should be asking you that."

Frankie's one cheekbone was bruised, there was

a contusion along the side of her jaw and her arm was in a sling. He gently took her chin in his hand and studied her eyes. "You okay? Has anyone checked you out?"

Her gaze was curious. "Paige did because everyone else was busy. But what about you, T? You don't look so good."

Ty's automatic response was that he was fine, but he wasn't. Not by a long shot. *Not by* any *shot, dammit.* He sighed and shoved a hand through his hair. "I'm just peachy."

Frankie looked like she didn't believe him. Not surprising, considering he felt like he'd been punched in the head.

"Really? Because you look like you just lost your best friend."

He wasn't ready to think about what was really bugging him, let alone talk about it. And certainly not with Frankie. "What I didn't like was getting a call to say that there'd been an accident and that Paige— But you were there too and I'm glad to see you're okay. You are okay, aren't you?"

"Yeah, nothing a hot soak in the tub won't fix." She was silent for a couple of beats. "So who called?"

"Nate," Ty admitted, and as he was looking right

at Frankie, he couldn't miss the abrupt change that came over her. Her back stiffened, her eyes instantly cooled and her mouth curled into a sneer.

"Can't believe the big man actually took time off from his busy schedule to care about people he had no problem forgetting when he became a fancy Navy SEAL."

Ty, suitably distracted from his own disturbing thoughts, sighed. "Frankie," he said, slinging an arm across her shoulders and hugging her to his side. He pressed his lips to her temple. "When are you going to get over whatever has you riled up over Nate?"

"When hell freezes over," was her instant reply, but before she shrugged off his arm she laid her head against his shoulder in an affectionate gesture. "And you can tell him that too." She stalked off a few paces before turning. "But I have a piece of advice for you too, T," she said walking backwards. "This place is a madhouse and Paige is hurting more than she's letting on. Go help her."

He wordlessly held up his cast and Frankie sneered for the second time in as many minutes.

"Since when did something like a broken hand ever stop you?" she demanded. "The Tyler Reese I knew climbed down a cliff face with a fractured ankle to rescue me when I was fifteen. Man up, T, and see what's right in front of your nose." And with that piece of baffling advice she spun away and disappeared around the next corner.

CHAPTER TWELVE

PAIGE PAUSED AND scanned the notes in front of her. "Just give me the Cliff Notes version, Beth, and ignore the bruises. That's all they are, bruises."

"All right," the RN said on a sigh, gently bumping shoulders with Paige in unspoken support. "The patient was brought in fifteen minutes ago with tachycardia, tachypnea and a low-grade fever. EMTs had difficulty keeping him conscious and ventilated. We immediately drew bloods and bagged him but we're still waiting for the results."

"Any signs of injury?" Paige asked, hoping they weren't dealing with an abused baby because if that happened it might spark the flood of emotion she was bottling up behind a thin veneer of professionalism. If that dam broke she'd probably cry about everything that had happened over the past twenty years.

"Nothing except a recent spider bite that he was

treated for, and, believe me," the RN admitted in a low voice, "we looked."

"Okay, I'll examine him but you might want to get a trolley with a paeds CL insertion and electrodes. Oh, and see if there's an ECHO available," she called out when Beth hurried off, pausing to check the next sheet before pushing open the door to ER 4.

Bryce and Courtney Cavendish hovered close to the bed, looking terrified as a nursing assistant worked on keeping the toddler ventilated. Dressed in just a disposable diaper, little Joshua looked tiny and fragile on the large ER bed.

Despite having being bagged, Paige could see that his breathing was fast and erratic, and instead of looking flushed, as one would expect in a child running a fever, his skin was pale, almost translucent.

"Good evening," she said, entering the room with a calm professional smile. "I'm Dr. Carlyle."

They turned as one and their reaction instantly reminded Paige of her bruised face. "Just ignore the bruises," she said on a little laugh. "I had a little mishap this afternoon. So," she continued briskly, "when did you first notice Joshua's symptoms?"

Paige listened intently as she gently examined the toddler and was probing his head and shoulders for trauma when he suddenly jerked and opened his eyes, giving her the opportunity to watch his pupil reaction.

She knew the instant he realized that she was someone strange because fear and confusion flashed across his little face. It crumpled and he opened his mouth to cry just as his eyes rolled back in his head.

Courtney rushed to the bed looking like she wanted to gather her son into her arms but her husband wrapped his arms around her and drew her away with a murmured, "Let them do their job, honey."

"Oh, God." Courtney turned and wept quietly into her husband's throat and Paige tried not to feel envious of their obvious love for each other and their child. What must it be like to have that kind of unspoken, unwavering support?

"He's all right," Courtney continued to sob. "Our baby's going to be all right." She turned wet, hopeful eyes on Paige. "He's going to be all right, isn't he?"

Paige winced inwardly. How did you tell a child's distraught mother that you had no idea what was wrong with him and that he might need some invasive procedures to get those answers? Procedures that could be both painful and dangerous.

"I promise that we'll get to the bottom of Joshua's problem," she said gently, knowing she couldn't in all good conscience tell the terrified woman what she wanted to hear. "Before I ask you and your husband to go with Nurse Bremner, I'd like to ask you a few questions."

"Of c-course," the young father said, looking white and shaky as though he understood what Paige wasn't saying. Her heart squeezed and she instinctively knew they weren't dealing with abuse. These parents obviously loved and cared for their son. The trick now was to fix little Joshua as soon as possible so his parents could take him home where he belonged.

Intent on the Cavendishes, Paige was only vaguely aware of a large presence coming up behind her and it was several moments before she realized it was Ty. Studiously ignoring the prickles of awareness marching up and down her spine, she concentrated instead on her questions.

Besides, she had no idea what he was still doing there and couldn't afford to care. Not with the crisis they were facing, and not with her heart. She needed to concentrate and wished he would go away. *Far, far away.* Now instead of next week. Now before she got in any deeper.

He waited until the young couple left with the nurse to take over the bagging.

"I thought you'd left," Paige said briskly, sending him a brief glance as she checked the toddler's pupil reaction again.

"I'll wait around until you're ready to leave."

"It might be late," she warned absently, frowning as something caught her eye. "In fact, you should go. This is going to take a while. I'll get a taxi."

"I'm not leaving," he growled irritably.

But he was. He was leaving next week and he hadn't told her. In fact, he hadn't said much of anything, let alone the important stuff. Blocking out her thoughts was difficult with a headache but she leaned closer to Joshua and gently pressed her fingers to the boy's neck. "Mmm." She whipped her stethoscope from around her neck and fitted them to her ears as she pressed the disk over Joshua's chest. "Did anyone else notice that?"

"Notice what?" the NA asked, leaning closer. "What did you see, Dr. Carlyle?"

"Where's the blood work?" Paige asked as she gently palpated the boy's chest, ignoring the pain shooting up her arm from her injured wrist because she could hear a dull sound and that was never a good thing. "We need those results." She turned to the NA. "Put a rush on them, Stacey. If it's what I think it is, this little boy's in trouble."

"What—?"

"Results. Please. Here," she said, thrusting the stethoscope at Ty. "If you won't leave then tell me what you hear." After a brief pause, Ty took the scope and moved beside her, silent as he slid the disk over the tiny chest. Paige held her breath.

"Dammit, Ty," she burst out after a long pause. "Tell me you hear it too."

Despite her earlier wish that he'd leave so she could start getting over him, she was abruptly glad he hadn't. All other qualified personnel were occupied and if she was right about her patient, they couldn't afford to wait.

"Heart rate is dropping," she murmured, "but so are blood saturation levels." Paige eyed the monitor with concern. Saturation levels were a lot lower than they'd been ten minutes earlier despite the PPV. And Joshua, who'd again come around, had begun to hiccup and his crying was weak.

"Hmm," Ty murmured. "Lung auscultation reveals coarse crackles while the heart appears... muffled." He removed the stethoscope and looped it around Paige's neck. "I think you're right. What's your take?"

The question put him inches away. "With the slight jugular vein enlargement, decreased saturation levels, bradycardia and hiccups...dammit, all it can be is a—"

"Tamponade," they said simultaneously, and Paige's shoulders slumped. She'd hoped he would come to a different conclusion but wasn't surprised he hadn't. Little Joshua was in cardiac tamponade, a dangerous condition that occurred when the sac around the heart filled with fluid, putting pressure on the organ and preventing normal functioning. When that became too much, one or more chambers sometimes collapsed.

It was often fatal.

"Okay. What do you want me to do?" Ty asked quietly, his gaze intent on hers and not offering advice she hadn't requested in deference to her official status as the doctor in charge.

The question surprised her. For a trauma surgeon who liked taking charge, he was being remarkably restrained. She didn't have time to wonder why.

Absently rubbing her aching temple, she spied the sonar machine. "I need a better look," she said, hurrying over to the equipment. "And I don't have time to wait for an ECHO."

"Fluoroscope?" Ty asked, referring to a very expensive machine that worked like a real-time X-ray.

Paige snorted. "You're kidding, right? You do remember that this is the wilds of Washington and not some fancy LA clinic?"

He stared at her for a long moment before sighing. "You're doing it the old-fashioned way, then." And Paige stilled.

Oh, yeah, she reminded herself, *you're the primary on this one. It's up to you to see the Cavendishes get to take their son home.*

"You've done it before?" he asked quietly.

Paige paused before saying, "Not on an infant. Please, tell me you've done this on an infant?"

"Nope, sorry."

"Oh, boy." She looked up and their eyes locked, and just for an instant everything fell away. With difficulty she forced herself to ask, "Can you, um...?" but he held up his injured hand and Paige realized how much she'd hoped he would offer to do it.

"I'm also not registered to practice in Washington, Paige. You know that."

She did. She knew that but they needed someone experienced—preferably with full use of both hands.

"Listen," he said quietly. "With the NA we have two pairs of hands among us. I'll talk you through it."

She paused, knowing that he was right. He had the experience and she had the dominant hand in working order. "Pulse dropping to seventy, Paige," he announced, with a sharp look that said he was waiting for her decision. "And he's showing signs of cyanosis."

Snapping into action, Paige grabbed a tube of gel to squirt a generous amount on her tiny patient's chest.

"Keep bagging him," she urged the NA, noting the definite signs that the toddler wasn't getting enough oxygen as she located his heart with the probe. She sucked in a breath when the organ popped into view on the screen.

"Marked pericardial effusion with evidence of early cardiac tamponade," Paige muttered. "Dammit, it's worse than I thought. Maybe we can get him up to OR—"

"There's no time," Ty interrupted, pointing to the top of the heart where the right chamber appeared to be slightly squashed. "Do it now before he arrests."

Paige sucked in a deep breath. "You're right," she muttered, before saying briskly, "Stacey, we need twenty-five ug per minute of dopamine and one point two mg furesomide, una tantum, while I prep him for a pc. Where the hell is Beth? *Dammit*, I need five mils of two percent lidocaine, a twenty-two-gauge pericardiocentesis needle with guide and dilators, a scalpel, pigtail catheter and a vacuum bag." She sent Ty a quick look. "If you're serious about assisting, I'm going to need pediatric electrodes and an iodine swab."

Working quickly, Paige injected a sedative directly into the drip-line port, and opened the line.

"We need a forty-five-degree angle of elevation," she began, but Ty was already working the levers with his feet. Beth finally returned and Paige instantly directed her to the bed. "Make sure he doesn't move, Beth. I want him absolutely still for this," she said, moving into position with a quick prayer.

So many things could go wrong with such a tiny patient.

"You'll do fine," Ty said calmly, correctly interpreting her hesitation. "Just breathe deeply and focus. I know your wrist hurts. Block it off and… That's good," he said when she'd sucked in a deep breath and let it out. "Now take another and let it out slowly while you decide what you need to do." He held out the large-gauge needle attached to a twenty-ml syringe and a scalpel.

She reminded herself that he was used to taking control, that he was the one usually giving orders. Yet here he was easily letting her take the lead without attempting to influence her.

Paige took the scalpel with her left hand and gave a wince. "You okay?" he asked as she transferred it to her right hand. She nodded, and spared him a look. "Good," he said crisply. "That's good. An incision will make the cannula insertion easier. Make a half-inch incision at the point where the left costal margin meets the xiphisternum. Great," he added after Paige made the cut.

"Now…introduce the needle and dissect the subcutaneous tissue. You'll feel a small pop when you pierce the wall," he murmured calmly, maneuvering the sonar probe to give Paige a clearer image of the heart with its inferior fluid-filled sac.

"Right, now angle it towards the left shoulder at a twenty—no, sharper, Paige, you don't want to damage the internal mammary artery or the neurovascular bundle on the inferior rib surface. There, that's it...perfect. Okay, now gently pull back on the plunger as you aim for the left shoulder tip...*slowly*...there, see on the monitor? The needle tip is about an inch from the sac. Just a fraction more," he breathed into the tense silence that had settled over the ER room, a silence broken only by his murmured words and the slow, irregular beeping of the heart monitor.

Calm had settled over Paige. She'd pushed the pain to the back of her mind and concentrated instead on breathing as Ty had instructed. Her ribs hurt with every inhalation but she soon realized that her breathing had slowed to sync with his.

She didn't know if he'd done it purposely but it felt like they'd entered a vacuum where everything—the room, the world and even her abused body—faded. Her hands seemed to be connected to his mind, already doing his bidding before he could voice his thoughts. It was a strange yet exhilarating experience to be so attuned to another person that you knew, even before they spoke, what they were thinking.

"Excellent...perfect positioning. Now...wait for the... Okay, hold steady for the flashback then carefully fill the syringe."

All eyes watched the monitor as the syringe filled.

"It's cloudy," Ty murmured, and though she wanted to look, she kept her eyes on the screen. Any movement on her part could cause the needle to penetrate the heart and put her patient in cardiac arrest.

Then the monitor stopped beeping.

Paige froze. Had she done something wrong?

Ty murmured for her to wait. It had to be the longest seconds of Paige's life but after a few hair-raising moments, the beeping resumed and she released her breath on a gusty exhalation of relief.

"Cardiac rhythm is already normalizing," Ty murmured. "What's next?"

"Guide wire," she said shakily, trying awkwardly to remove the syringe from the needle. Finally Beth took over, quickly twisting it free. "Thanks. Get it up to the lab, will you? I want a full analysis by morning. Be sure to request a fungal test and I want to check clotting parameters so we can correct any abnormalities while we wait."

With deft movements, she inserted the guide wire through the needle until it entered the pericardium. Once she'd removed the needle, she passed a soft-tipped pigtail catheter over the wire until it too entered the pericardium. She slid the wire free and connected the vacuum bag, finally securing the incision site with a couple of small stitches and tape.

When there was nothing more to do, she stepped back to check the monitor. "Looks promising," she murmured to herself as relief began to flood through her, along with all the myriad aches and pains she'd ignored during the procedure. "Heart and respiration rates rising…sinus rhythm returning…and, wow!" She gusted out a shaky breath as her lips curved involuntarily. "Look at that. His color's better too."

They'd done it and it wouldn't have been possible without Ty and his calming presence—without his firm, quiet instruction. He was too good, too knowledgeable a physician to lose because he was mad at the world.

"Stacey, call upstairs and let them know he's on his way. I want to keep him sedated until we know more. Beth, put a rush on those samples while I talk to mom and dad."

When the nurses had left, the only sound in the room was the quiet beeping of the machine and Paige's heart pounding in her ears. She needed a minute.

No, maybe two, because her head suddenly swam, pounding out of control, along with her heart. Every bruise seemed to have a pulse of its own too and she felt each throb as if for the first time. She must have swayed because Ty was suddenly there, supporting her.

"Dammit, Paige—"

The door opened and, conscious of the picture they made, Paige quickly stepped away and turned to meet Joshua's parents. They were visibly upset by the sight of their son, hooked up to monitors and with a tube sticking out of his chest. Paige drew them aside to explain and by the time her little patient had been whisked away to ICU it was all she could do to walk to the door.

She hurt. All over. Including her heart.

Ty was waiting outside and the instant she stepped into the corridor he gently took her arm. "You're done," he said, slipping the lab coat and stethoscope off her.

She was a little surprised to find him still there. "I have a patient," she began, only to be interrupted by the shift supervisor.

"He's right, Paige," Marc Wallace said, coming up behind her. Her boss looked as though he'd been through the wringer. "You're done for the day and I don't want to see you till Monday."

"But—"

"Look at you," he said gently but firmly. "You can hardly stay on your feet. I'll get Kara Grant to take over the boy's care but from what I hear you did all the hard stuff." He reached out to squeeze her shoulder, murmuring an apology when she winced. "You saved a little boy's life, Paige, now let your man take you home."

Paige wanted to tell him that Ty wasn't her man but before she could get the words out, Marc was gone and Ty was steering her towards the exit.

Aware of the deep trembling in her core, Paige was silent on the drive home. Other than a few concerned looks, Ty too said nothing. Exhausted and hurting, the last thing she wanted to deal with was his leaving.

He parked and helped her out the SUV but when he tried to steer her towards his unit, Paige shook her head. She wanted to be surrounded by her own stuff and sleep in her own bed tonight. Besides, it was time she got used to being alone again.

Without arguing, Ty let her into her house and switched on the lights. It had been days since she'd actually spent any time there and the place felt empty.

Yep, a little voice drawled in her head. *As empty as your heart is going to be when he leaves.* But Paige wasn't going to think about that now. She just wanted to sleep. Maybe until her life got back to normal or she woke up and realized the past couple of months had been nothing but a pleasant dream.

Besides, talking clearly hadn't got her anywhere so far.

She headed for the stairs and when he came up behind her she turned to stare at him dully. The overhead light cast most of his features in shadow, illuminating only one side of his face. His eyes were dark and unreadable and his mouth unsmiling.

She couldn't stop her gaze from dropping to study its sculpted lines or keep from recalling exactly how it felt on hers. Especially the kiss in ER. It had confused her as much as it had sent her heart skittering because he'd kissed her as if she was delicate and precious to him. But it was a lie. Like his lie of omission.

"I told you I'm not leaving," he growled softly. "And I meant it."

Too tired and heartsick to tell him what she already knew, Paige turned and slowly took the stairs. She concentrated on lifting each foot because her muscles had stiffened and it was an effort to move.

At the landing she headed for the bathroom, vaguely conscious of Ty disappearing into her bedroom. She turned the shower to steaming and had to sit on the bath to remove her shoes. It took a concentrated effort but she'd managed to unlace one sneaker before two masculine hands and a dark head appeared in her vision.

He brushed her hands aside and finished the job of undressing her. Then he stripped and drew her into the shower.

Tears pricked the backs of her eyes and she gulped them down. She couldn't—just couldn't—bear memories of him in here too. "Ty," she began, but he gently soothed her and closed the door.

"Let me, Paige," he murmured against her temple. "Let me take care of you."

And though she surrendered—mostly because

she didn't have the energy to resist—Paige knew he didn't really mean it. But that was okay. She'd had enough experience taking care of herself.

She didn't know how long he let the hot water work on her abused muscles, but resting against his hard warm body she drifted, only to stir when he carefully ran the soapy sponge over her. Once her skin was pink—where she wasn't black and blue—he tugged her from the shower, dried her and pulled a huge T-shirt over her head.

She began floating and it took her a couple of seconds to realize that he was carrying her. The comforter had already been pulled back and within seconds of him gently tucking her in, everything slipped away.

Sometime later she was roused from a disturbing dream where she was standing on the rocky shoreline, watching a figure disappear into the fog. She must have been crying because Ty's hands were soothing and her face was wet.

She pried her eyes open and blinked in the low light. Shirtless and with his hair mussed, he looked big and bad and dangerous in her girly room.

"Hey," he murmured. "You okay?"

"Yeah," she croaked, rolling over and wincing when her body protested. "Ouch. Why?"

He helped her up. "You were crying. Bad dream?"

"Hmm," she said noncommittally, unwilling to recall the devastation she'd felt in her dream or what it might mean. "How's…um… Joshua?"

"He's fine. Vitals stable." He held out his hand. Two small tablets nestled in his palm. "Take these," he said, handing her a glass of water.

Wordlessly she swallowed them, easing her body down into the bed when he took the glass from her. She was just slipping into sleep when she jolted.

"Ty?"

"Right here," he murmured from somewhere close.

The sound of his voice had her body relaxing. "But you won't be," she murmured sadly.

"Won't be what, babe?"

Babe. She knew she should be protesting but she liked it. "Be here."

"I'm right here," he soothed, running a hand down her arm. "I'm not leaving you tonight."

But he would. And soon. "I know, you know," she murmured, feeling her throat close when he smoothed a strand of hair off her face.

"Know what?"

She silently enjoyed the gentle caress for a few moments before admitting, "That you're leaving."

When Paige next woke, the sun was high and the bed was empty. As empty as the house felt. And when she went next door, she found that empty too and tried not to care.

He'd promised he would be there but he'd lied. Just as her mother had fifteen years ago when she'd promised a frightened pre-teen that she would never leave her.

CHAPTER THIRTEEN

TY STARED AT the rolling lawns of his mother's manicured gardens and wished he was a thousand miles away. He lifted the wineglass to his mouth and grimaced. The Chablis was perfectly fine but he'd have preferred whiskey or beer. Always had, despite his mother's efforts to turn him into what she called a "civilized man".

Somehow she'd found out he was back in LA and had issued a dinner invitation. Ty knew a summons when he heard it and hadn't been surprised to find she'd invited the daughter of an acquaintance to dinner. The woman was as perfectly nice as the Chablis but Ty kept comparing her to the one woman he couldn't seem to get out of his head.

What had surprised him was his mother's latest companion. Paul Richmond was well heeled and well educated but, unlike her previous husbands, he could hardly be called polished, sophisticated and smug. And because he wasn't, Ty had liked him instantly. However, he wasn't in the mood for a dinner party and he wasn't in the mood for his mother's brand of matchmaking or interrogation—which the evening was actually a cover for.

The week since his return had been jam-packed with meetings and appointments, mostly to keep him from thinking. It hadn't worked, because all he'd done *was* think.

About Paige, about her accident, and about the mind-numbing terror he'd felt when he'd thought she'd been seriously hurt.

He shook off the disturbing images that had constantly been on his mind since that day—images that had followed him even in sleep—because if he thought too much about them he might have to admit that he'd been an idiot.

That leaving Paige had been the biggest mistake of his life.

One minute he'd been watching her sleep, the next...

Okay, so maybe he'd freaked out a little. He'd experienced a crushing feeling in his chest that had had him staggering from the room, thinking he'd been having a heart attack. He'd gone looking for brandy and had found a six-pack of his favorite beer instead. Beer she had to have bought for him because she *was* a wine drinker.

His world had tilted alarmingly and he'd felt as though he'd been rushing towards disaster without a brake. Without a single thought to the consequences.

It was that last notion that had scared him the most. That he knew where this was going and simply didn't care.

So he'd done the one thing he knew would get his life back on track. The one thing he'd gone to Washington to find.

Control of his life.

And while Paige had slept he'd bumped up his flight, packed in record time and left before she could wake because he knew if she looked at him with huge exotic eyes that drew him in against his will, he'd willingly go under for the third time.

A hundred times since then he'd assured himself that escaping from her had saved his life, so why did it feel as though there was a huge empty hole in his soul and that he was slowly suffocating?

A couple of days ago he'd seen his specialist and though he was still mostly uncertain if his hand would ever withstand the rigors of surgery, he hadn't felt much of anything when Peter Dawson had claimed he'd healed well and with therapy might even get back his former dexterity.

The news should have pleased him but all he could think about was the tentative relationship he'd been forging with his father and about reconnecting with Nate. Relationships he'd left behind.

And in the dark hours of the night he lay awake thinking about Paige and wondering. If she was okay, what she was doing and who she was doing it with. A million times he'd caught himself turning to tell her something or he'd reach for his phone only to realize that she wasn't there and that he'd given up the right to call.

He'd left her curled into her pillows, for God's sake; left her bruised and hurting and needing someone to lean on while he'd slipped out like a thief in the night.

He'd called Frankie, but other than to tell him he was scum she refused to take his calls. But only after telling him that Paige was over him and dating again.

Dating?

His gut clenched for about the trillionth time since he'd heard. *Well, hell.*

And suddenly he could stand it no longer. He had to get away from the stifling atmosphere of his mother's house and the smog and traffic of LA. It had taken him over a week to realize what he hadn't as a kid. He could breathe in Washington and it had nothing—or almost nothing—to do with the fresh air.

It had to do with the people. His father, Jack, Nate and Frankie...and now a sweet, feisty, bossy pain-in-the-ass distraction he couldn't stop thinking about and needed more than his next breath.

With a muttered oath he slammed down the glass on the nearest surface and headed for the door, only to be stopped by his mother's peremptory, "Tyler, why don't you tell us when you're going back to St Augustine's? I hear they've been horribly short-handed since you buried yourself in the wilderness."

"I'm not going back, Mother," he said impatiently, because his mother refused to admit that his injury might put a permanent damper on his meteoric surgical career. A career she liked to tell everyone about. "And Port St. John's is hardly the wilderness."

"What do you mean, you're not going back?" she demanded, ignoring everything else.

"I resigned." He hadn't but that was his next step. He was going back to Washington.

He was finally going home.

Renée gasped and paled. "But…but why, for heaven's sake?" She rose off the couch looking both elegant and cool, the perfect line of her brow marred by a wrinkle of displeasure. She might be sixty-two but looked fifty and was still beautiful. "That's so typically reckless and short-sighted of you, Tyler. I thought you'd outgrown that juvenile behavior but it seems spending time with that man, in that Godforsaken place, has turned you against me again."

"Mother—" he began wearily, only to be interrupted by a cold, "You'll regret it. I certainly did. Besides, I have it on excellent authority that you'll make a full recovery and when you do—"

"When I do, Mother, it might not be as a surgeon."

"Of course it will, darling, and St. Augustine's will take you back. Dr. Hudson assured me of that."

Furious that his mother had been discussing him with the hospital administrator, he said flatly, "It's done. I've put my house on the market."

Renée gasped and slapped a hand over her heart as though he'd stabbed her in the chest. "Oh, my God. You're moving to Washington, aren't you?

You're throwing away everything you've worked so hard to achieve. And for what? A rundown harbor town with a second-rate hospital?"

"Yes," Ty said quietly, firmly. "I am. And Port St. John's is hardly run-down. In fact, it's tripled in size in the last twenty years and is a hugely popular tourist resort town. And *that man,* as you call him, is my father." He turned to walk out the door.

"You'll regret this silly decision, Tyler, just as I did."

"No, Mother, I won't," he said quietly over his shoulder. "What I regret is not doing it sooner."

Over his mother's spluttered protest he heard Paul Richmond say, "Let him go, Renée. His mind's clearly made up." And just before he closed the front door he heard Paul add, "Besides, the boy's in love."

His mind instantly rejected being called a boy almost as much as those last words. He actually scoffed as he slammed the front door behind him.

He'd just realized that he belonged in Washington, that's all. Nothing hearts-and-roses about that. Just a hankering for the town of his birth and spending time with his father, with Nate. And with Paige, too, he admitted.

If she ever spoke to him again.

Satisfied that he'd cleared up that misconception in his own mind, he slid behind the wheel of his shiny sports car and froze as everything abruptly fell into place—like the cogs of a safe lock tumbling into place.

It was as if an inner door swung open, revealing... Ty swore, his chest squeezing and his gut churning just like it had the night of Paige's accident. With a blinding flash of insight he realized that all the emotions bombarding him that night, tonight—every moment since—were none other than...

Oh, God, he could barely think the word, let alone say it. But there was no denying his feelings. He was...*yeah, that,* with a woman who'd wormed her way into his heart, first by knocking him out cold and then with every smile, every scowl and every blush since then. A woman who faced her problems head on instead of running from them. A woman he suddenly couldn't see himself living without.

There was no getting away from the truth.

He loved Paige Carlyle and wanted her in his life.

He'd just have to convince her to renegotiate

their deal, that's all. A deal that would last the rest of their lives.

Firing up the engine, Ty whipped out of his mother's driveway and headed for the southbound freeway, his mouth curving in a wolfish grin. His little faerie commando had better watch her six because Ty was planning a sneak attack. And he knew exactly how surgically precise and devious it was going to be.

His feisty little medic—aka Dr. Cutie—didn't stand a chance.

Paige heard music as she drifted up through layers of sleep and caught herself smiling before she remembered that her life sucked. Oh, yeah. It was the first time she'd actually managed to fall asleep without tossing and turning because she missed having a big warm body to curl into.

Maybe she should get a dog, she thought sleepily. A huge big shaggy dog. One that she could take for long walks on the beach and curl up with on a cold rainy night. One who would always be happy to see her and wouldn't disappear in the middle of the night and break her freaking heart.

Yep, she yawned, snuggling into the pillow she was wrapped around. A dog sounded great—

Her eyes popped open and she froze as two things registered at once. One, the music was closer than she'd thought and, two—*oh, boy*—her pulse charged ahead of her brain because... because someone was moving around downstairs.

Her eyes widened incredulously.

You have got to be kidding me.

What the heck were the statistics of that happening twice?

Well, she thought furiously, flinging back the covers and grabbing her trusty flashlight off the bedside table. This time there would be no mercy. This time she would not—*not, you hear, Paige Deborah Carlyle?*—let a sexy BAB render her stupid.

Narrowing her eyes, she firmed her lips and tightened her grip. *This* guy was going down and *this* time she would make sure he stayed down. She wouldn't call the cops because Frankie had said she would help her bury the body.

Paige knew *just* the place.

Halfway down the stairs she froze because her heart was pounding so hard she felt a little light-headed and...and there was a warm glow of—she leaned over the banister—candles?...coming from the sitting room.

Music and *candles? What the hell?*

Okay, so clearly her intruder hadn't heard that stealth was a major requirement of "intruding".

Scowling fiercely because she'd taken down the last one with her awesome ninja skills, Paige marched down the stairs prepared to give the guy a piece of her mind. She was the sister of a Navy SEAL, she told herself, *and* a Top Gun. She was—

A huge dark shape materialized beside her and acting on instinct she swung the flashlight with all her strength.

She heard a low oath as it connected and before she knew it she'd been pinned against the wall and disarmed. Shocked by the speed with which it had happened, Paige opened her mouth and... screamed.

Oh, yeah. Killer ninja skills to the rescue.

She thought she heard, "For God's sake, Paige, it's me," but it was probably her imagination because Ty was gone. He'd snuck out when she'd been down and out and she was *never*—she thrust a leg between two long muscled ones and hooked an ankle—*letting anyone*—rammed the heel of her hand into his gut—*hurt her*—and growled with satisfaction when she heard a grunt of pain as her attacker let her go—*ever again!*

She shoved hard and the next instant the earth shook. She uttered a loud *"Haaai ya!"* as he went down hard.

There was a stunned silence, a muttered, "What the—?" in a voice that was both familiar and as unexpected as the snort the intruder uttered with his next breath. The snort turned into a chuckle and soon deep belly laughs filled the entrance and rattled the panes. It took a couple of dozen heart-beats to realize that—

"Ty?"

When the man on the floor continued to laugh like a lunatic, Paige stomped over to the wall and hit the lights. And there, on the floor where she'd tossed him—okay, it had been more of a shove—was Tyler Reese, dressed in nothing but a pair of worn, faded jeans and a wrist brace. Looking even better than she remembered.

It took another couple of seconds for her brain to compute and when it did, she snapped her mouth closed, narrowed her eyes and stomped closer, snatching the flashlight off the floor where it had rolled.

"Try anything funny and it's lights out," she snarled, scowling down at him, one hand on her hip, the other brandishing her trusty flash. She didn't know what the hell was so damn funny but he took one look at her and whooped with freaking hilarity until, seething with frustration and the remnants of adrenaline, she tried to kick him.

His hand shot out and grabbed her foot and the next thing she knew she'd landed on him hard enough to knock the breath from her lungs. Her bruised ribs protested but before *she* could punch him, he'd rolled and had her pinned beneath him.

She opened her mouth to berate him for manhandling her but Ty swooped down and caught the garbled protest with his mouth. Stunned and a little turned on, Paige tried to shove him away but he grabbed her hands and anchored them beside her head as he continued his assault on her mouth.

And her senses too, *dammit*.

The thought had her nipping his bottom lip hard enough that he broke the kiss and growled, "*Ouch.* What the hell was that for?"

Somehow one of his thighs had sneaked between hers and she could feel how turned on *he* was. The discovery was enough to lend her strength and she punched him once…twice before he grabbed her hands.

Pain shot through her sprained wrist, which had

to account for the tears suddenly blurring her vision. It also made her gasp and try to buck him off.

"Dammit," he growled, breathing hard, she was gratified to notice because she was huffing like a geriatric steam engine. "What's got into you?"

"You..." She gulped back a sob and glared at him accusingly. She tried to kick him but he had her legs pinned. "You...you *left*." Tears blinded her but she furiously blinked them away. No way was she giving him the satisfaction of crying over him. She wasn't. Her wrist hurt, her butt hurt and...and, damn him, her heart hurt too. "Without saying goodbye. Like I was a...a one-night stand, *dammit*."

She must have surprised him because he released her hands and Paige took advantage of his distraction to shove at him, scuttling away when he rolled over to blink at her stupidly.

Her back hit the wall and she instinctively drew her knees up. She recognized it as a defensive pose but she didn't want to be vulnerable to him again. And even though she'd known he was leaving, she'd been as devastated as when her mother had died.

"Hey," he said softly, and Paige realized he'd

peeled himself off the floor and was back-to-the wall beside her. His yummy smell enveloped her and she drew in a huge lungful before she could stop herself.

"I'm sorry," he murmured, thrusting a hand through his tousled hair in obvious frustration.

"For what, scaring the hell out of me for the second time?"

His mouth, mostly serious but often sensual—especially when he was contemplating kissing her—curved in amusement.

"No." He grimaced, all amusement gone. "For leaving like that. For being an idiot."

Instead of replying, she gave him a filthy look and *thunked* her head against the wall. After a couple of beats she felt him move and the next moment he was peering into her averted face.

Scowling, she shoved his shoulder.

"Go away, I'm over you."

"Is that why you tried to split my skull open again? Because I have to tell you," he continued when she just growled at him, "for the rest of my life I'll never forget the sight of you standing over me like an avenging faerie commando, ready to whoop my ass."

"I did whoop your ass," she reminded him

smartly, secretly pleased with his description. "I wasn't the one knocked on his ass by a girl."

He was silent a moment. "Yeah," he murmured. "I was, wasn't I?"

The tone of his voice aroused her curiosity and when she turned her head and caught him studying her as if he'd never seen her before, a confused frown wrinkled her brow.

"What?"

"You knocked me on my ass."

"I just said that."

"No," he murmured, lifting a hand to cup her jaw, and Paige stilled at the expression in his eyes. Her heart lurched and an entire swarm of locusts invaded her belly. "I mean you *really* knocked me on my ass."

Concerned that he might have hit his head, Paige said, "Ty…?" But he gave a low rough laugh and the next instant she found herself flat on the floor with his hard body covering hers.

Really concerned now, she blinked up into eyes the color of the late summer sky and her breath stuttered to a stop.

With his eyes on hers, he slid his hands into her hair to hold her still and with a soft, "You're awesome," slowly dipped his head to drop a kiss on her startled mouth.

On a muffled oath, he deepened the kiss until they were both breathing heavily and Paige felt just how much the wild mating of mouths had affected him.

Oh, boy. Her too.

He lifted his head long enough to announce, "I can't wait to tell our kids about this," before swooping back to feed her the hottest, hungriest kisses she'd ever experienced.

It was much later when she was sated and draped boneless across Ty's body that she roused herself enough to croak, "Our kids?"

"Hmm?" Ty hummed, smoothing a big hand down her back to her bottom.

"Just before you ravished me you said; 'I can't wait to tell our kids about this.'" She pushed herself up onto her elbow with great effort because she was still trembling from the storm of passion he'd unleashed on her. "Firstly, what the hell? And secondly, *what the hell*?"

He blinked as though waking from a deep sleep and after a long pause, during which his body tensed by degrees, he frowned. "You don't want to marry me?"

Stunned as much by his words as she was by the uncertainty in his tone, Paige gaped at him. After a couple of beats she sat up and reached for the USMC shirt she usually slept in, only to blink when it was whipped out of reach.

"Answer me."

"Well," she said carefully, beginning to get annoyed. "I don't know. You haven't asked me yet."

"But…" He thrust a hand through his hair and after a long pause his breath escaped in a long whoosh. "I'm jobless."

Startled, Paige could only blink.

"And I'm homeless."

Her eyes widened and she was only vaguely aware that her heart had begun a heavy pounding in her chest.

For a long moment he stared at her before reaching out to cup her face with his hands. "And… and you didn't just knock me on my ass, Paige. I fell hard. For you."

"What…?" She swallowed before trying again. "What are you saying, Ty?"

"I'm saying that I'm so in love with you that I'm prepared to beg."

"You…?" She shook her head as if to clear it. "You l-love *me*?"

"Yes," he murmured, kissing her gently on the nose. "You. The bossy pain-in-the-ass distraction I didn't want but need more than my next breath."

"But…what about your job? Your life?"

"It's here with you, Paige."

She was stunned speechless but after a couple of gasping breaths managed, "I… I—"

Chuckling, Ty pulled her into his arms. "I can't believe the only time I ever see you speechless is when I tell you I love you. Is it that surprising?"

"Well, no," she admitted with a growing smile, because who wouldn't grin knowing that the hottest guy in America had willingly entered her house and declared his love? "I am pretty awesome but—"

With a laugh Ty caught her mouth in a deep wet kiss that seemed to go on forever. Finally he broke away to murmur against her lips, "Yes, you are awesome. But you haven't answered my question."

Breathless, Paige traced his much-loved face and could not help herself from dropping a kiss on his mouth, his jaw and taking a nip out of his ear. "Which one was that?"

He pulled her away to look into her eyes. "Do you love me and will you marry me?"

"That's two—" she began, only to break off

with a startled squeak when he dipped his head and nipped her lip.

Curling her fingers in his hair, she yanked his head up so she could see his expression when she said, "Yes. And you'd better not tell our kids what I'm about to do next."

His grin was a mix of relief, joy and blinding love. "And what's that, Dr. Cutie?"

"This," she breathed, shoving him backwards. And when she was straddling him, Paige stared down at him with triumph. "I'm going to turn your world upside down."

* * * * *

*If you enjoyed this story, check out
these other great reads from
Lucy Ryder*

*CAUGHT IN A STORM OF PASSION
FALLING AT THE SURGEON'S FEET
TAMED BY HER ARMY DOC'S TOUCH
RESISTING HER REBEL HERO*

All available now!